Mackie's Men

By Lynn Ray Lewis

ISBN-10# 1-945012-26-9
ISBN-13# 978-1-945012-26-6

Edited by Vinvatar Publishing

Artwork by Jess Buffett Graphic Designs

Published by Vinvatar Publishing
Website: Vinvatar.com

Table of Contents

Chapter 1

Maxine Vaught was settling down with a bowl of popcorn and her e-reader. The day had been gloomy and misty rain had turned into a steady light rain. The weather girl said they would be having popup thunderstorms all night with wind chills just above freezing. All in all, it was a typical late March night, and she was glad to be home with the time to catch up on her reading and just relax. She loved the peace and quiet of her home sitting back from the gravel road and a half mile from any neighbors. Her little two bedroom bungalow was perfect for her and the grey cat that found its way from the dairy farm down the road to live with her.

She was on the third chapter of an intensely erotic book when she thought she heard a gunshot. Since the noise hadn't been repeated, she went back to the heroes of the book who were spanking their love interest into a sexual frenzy, just as one of the three men filled her with his overly large cock, she heard the loud boom again. It was followed by a crashing sound and she saw a bright light down by the road through her front window. "Dammit." Mackie got up, shut off her e-reader and went to the window. "I really don't want to go out there," she told the grey cat. She pushed her feet into her mud boots and grabbed her cell phone, her coat, and a throw blanket that she crocheted last winter.

She hopped on her golf cart and sped down the driveway, glad the trusty little vehicle had a sun top over her head that kept the rain from her face as she drove to the end of her driveway. Across the road from her property was a deep ravine filled with trees and a swiftly running stream that came from somewhere behind her property. She immediately saw what was burning and it scared the hell out of her. There was an SUV hung up in some of the young trees and the side was smashed in. She could hear a baby crying and a woman's hysterical voice yelling for Eric to wake up.

Mackie ran to the vehicle and took a minute to decide how to proceed while taking her cell phone out of her pocket and dialing 911. The connection was bad but she told them what had happened, and thought she at least got the street out before the line was dropped. "Sonofabitch, that's no help." She was still cursing under her breath as she gingerly approached the vehicle. She balanced on the trunks of the trees to get to the smashed remains of the vehicle and could smell gas.

The young man's face was covered in blood, and the airbag had deployed covering the blood with a fine powdery substance. While she checked his pulse on the side of his neck, she told the woman to please calm down, "My name is Mackie, what's your name?"

"Jenny."

"Okay, Jenny, are you hurt?" When the girl shook her head, Mackie breathed a sigh of relief. She looked in the backseat and couldn't see the baby's face, but from the amount of noise it was making, the baby was either hurt badly or was just scared from the wreck. The young woman tried to get out of her seatbelt but it was jammed, and she started to get worked up again, so Mackie had to get stern with her, "Sit still, the car is sitting on some trees and if you move too fast or shift your weight, the whole thing is going down into the ravine. I know you're upset and worried but you need to focus right now." She stared at the younger woman until she got a nod from her. "What is the man's name who was driving?"

"Er-Eric."

"Okay, good, Jenny. Now, Eric is alive, but I don't know where he is hurt and I only have this small flashlight to see with, so I need you to feel if his legs are trapped, can you do that?"

Jenny reached over to feel Eric's legs and the dashboard. "Su-sure. I d-don't think h-he is trapped," Jenny replied.

"Okay, thanks, Jenny, think you can get unbuckled?"

"Y-yes, I th-think so," Jenny's reply reflected the knock on her head she took. After a few attempts, Jenny was able to unbuckle her seatbelt.

"Good job, Jenny. What is your baby's name, sweetie?"

"Eric junior."

"Aww, precious. Now I'm going to get the baby out and put him in my vehicle. I will be right back for you, okay?" With a nod from Jenny, Mackie and Jenny worked together to break the side glass window out. Mackie got the baby out of the vehicle, and ran the car seat containing two-month-old baby Eric, to the safety of her golf cart and left him on the seat. The child had fallen asleep despite the rain and all the noise the women had made breaking the window out. She went back for Jenny, and had to pull her out of the same window behind the driver's seat. The woman's right wrist was already swelling and her left foot looked like it might be broken or badly sprained. Mackie was just glad she was alive. She pulled and fell down on the tree branches, as she finally got Jenny to safety on the little cart with her son.

When she went back for the driver, she knew this one was going to be difficult to remove from the wreckage. A crowbar wasn't going to pry the door open and she still needed to double check with 911 to make sure they received the address. So she climbed through the back window and almost got her wide hips stuck, but with a few wiggles and she was certain a few cuts, she finally worked her way into the vehicle with the unconscious man. She loosened his seatbelt and pulled him from his seat onto the console, and had to sit for a few precious seconds to take a needed rest before tackling his weight again. He was well over six feet tall, and in the darkness she couldn't see his face very well. She imagined that even had it been daylight, between all the blood trickling from his head wound and the powder from the airbag, she wouldn't have gotten a good look at his face until he was cleaned up.

She looked at the width of the man's shoulders and knew she would never get him through that window. So she crawled through the back to the hatch and was grateful that after only a few kicks it popped open. Her foot was in the way when it tried to bounce back shut so at least she felt lucky for that. Pulling and yanking his dead weight over the backseat was impossible, until she found the latch that lowered the seat, to make the entire rear end of the vehicle cargo friendly. By the time she had him out of the vehicle and on the gravel road she was exhausted. The muscles in her arms were burning and trembling from the effort it took just to move him a few inches. Now the question was what to do with him?

The baby was crying again and Jenny was trying to soothe him. Mackie made up her mind and left Eric laying on the side of the road with her flashlight while she took Jenny and the baby back up to her house and let them inside. Once they were in the house, she hurried back to retrieve the unconscious young man. The rain had washed most of the powder coated blood from his face by the time she got to him and she could see that he was a very handsome young man. Even pale as death the man was good looking and she hoped he would be all right. She was pulling him up into the golf cart when he groaned and she started talking to him. "Eric, I am Mackie and you have been in an accident, I need you to help me get you into the house, okay?"

He continued to groan, but unable to move on his own, and she was losing the battle to get him on the seat. "Come on, Eric, I have Jenny and the baby in the house and Jenny needs you, you need to help me here. Just try to move your legs please? I'm a big girl but you are a lot bigger than me, and I can't help you by myself, Jenny needs you at the house." Mackie gave thanks when the man moved his legs trying to help her get his body on the cart. Finally, he was half sitting and half lying on the seat and she propped him up the best she could and slid into the driver's side and drove them to the house.

By the time she got the small family situated in her second bedroom and had gotten them cleaned up, warmed up and now asleep, she was ready to collapse herself. There was definitely something strange about the wreck and the people involved. She slipped out the backdoor to put away the golf cart, but decided to go back down to the wreck and see if she could find the baby's diaper bag and maybe Jenny's purse. She climbed into the vehicle through the back hatch and found the diaper bag and the purse, and as she trained the flashlight around the interior of the vehicle she spied a pistol and a wallet. She checked the glove box and found the registration to the vehicle and insurance papers. When she unfolded a long paper, she was a little surprised to see it was a marriage certificate dated a few days ago. Mackie stuffed the vehicle papers and everything else she gathered into the purse and diaper bag, then shut the door as she exited the wreck. Lightning and thunder were crashing and lighting up the landscape while she drove back to the house and parked in the lean-to. She took everything into the house and locked the door behind her.

She went into her bedroom and found the grey cat curled up on her bed asleep. The little creature made her smile. She wasn't a guard dog but she kept the house free of mice and other vermin and she was good company most of the time with her acrobatics. Mackie stripped her soaking wet clothes from her cold body and tossed on a pair of sweats. The fleece felt warm on her skin. She took her wet clothing into the laundry alcove and tossed it in the washer with the young couple's clothes and turned it on. She had loaned Jenny a nightgown, which the young woman had to hold up the hemline to walk without tripping, but at least it was warm. And the man, Eric, had been lying in bed in a pair of her cartoon pajama bottoms that came about six inches too short for his long legs but at least he was covered.

When Mackie went into the kitchen she saw Eric sitting at the table, he must have woke up and came to check out the place. She saw him rummaging through his wife's purse, and assumed he was looking for a cell phone. "I don't have a landline, all I have is a cell phone and it doesn't have a strong enough signal to call 911 in this storm, I tried." The item that he held in his hand was not a phone like she thought, it was just a little black box with a small green light and when he pressed the button the light turned red. He put it back into the purse and asked.

"Could I bother you for a cup of coffee or something hot? I am so damn cold I need to warm up inside and out."

"Sure, why don't you go into the living room and I'll get the pot started." She made the coffee, and grabbed the cream and sugar setting it next to the waiting mugs. She went to her room and dug out a t-shirt that might stretch across his wide shoulders and brought it to him on her way back to the kitchen to pour their coffee.

She put a teaspoon of sugar in his coffee and stirred it in the hot liquid, doctored her cup, and took both into the living room where Eric sat waiting. The t-shirt was a little tight but it covered his chest so it should make him feel a bit warmer. She took a lap rug and laid it over his shoulders much to his embarrassment. "Don't be a sissy, young man, you are cold, and I made the blankets for the sole purpose of keeping warm." She smiled at him and sat in her favorite overstuffed chair. They sipped the hot coffee and watched the lightning through her front windows. "You know, Eric, I am thirty years old and have seen some pretty messed up things in my life, so why don't you tell me why someone would shoot at you, and especially with a baby in the vehicle?" When he shook his head she didn't pressure him for the information. Not that she didn't want to know what was going on, but whatever it was, Eric wasn't inclined to share. Mackie sat quietly and watched him as if he was having an inner debate with himself.

He leaned forward, elbows on his knees, "Have you heard of a company by the name of Klinger, as in Klinger Corporation?" When she shook her head no he sighed. "Klinger Corporation has its fingers in a lot of different pies, I am in the Communications and Development Department. I just finished a new video gaming system that will blow the competition out of the water. One of our competitors tried to bribe a co-worker to steal the software for the system. Since I am a paranoid bastard I never left the software at the office. I think that's what this is all about." He sat back, sipped on his cooling coffee, and closed his eyes. "It never occurred to me that my wife and child meant so little that someone would rather kill me than allow the game to come online for the Christmas rush on sales."

"Klinger as in Eric and Jennifer Klinger?" At his look, Mackie had to tell him what she found. "Look, I was not really snooping, I went to get the diaper bag and Jenny's purse, and I found a pistol and took the papers from the glove box in case the gasoline I smelled caught on fire. The Marriage Certificate was there too." She got up and went to refresh her coffee taking his mug with her too and when she came back, "I haven't heard of the Klinger name before but I assume that it is a family business?" At his nod she said, "You can try to use my cell to call someone if you like. Maybe it will work now."

Eric was smiling and shook his head, "They will find me, I'm not worried. By the way, how did you get us out of the SUV?" Mackie knew he was changing the subject to get her off track. So she humored him and explained that she really had no idea how she did it. He watched her hands as she spoke, probably looking at the cuts that she had gotten from the broken windows in the vehicle.

She knew why his eyebrow kept arching as she related her part in rescuing his wife and baby, and going back for him. He saw a woman who was five foot ten in her bare feet and not a delicate little flower to look at. Mackie was built on the muscular side. Well, if she was honest, she was actually a bit chubby. She wore a size fourteen and had for most of her adult life. Men still introduced themselves to her considerable sized boobs instead of her eyes and although she learned to bring a finger up her middle for their eyes to follow so she could talk to them and not have to "say it through her breasts" during a conversation, she wasn't what you could call fat.

She tossed the clothes into the dryer and they talked, about anything but Eric's life. She told him about her plan to raise pheasants and quail for the markets. "I almost have enough saved for the barns to raise them in. I have been banking my money from my second job so by this time next year I hope to be raising birds full time." She laughed a little, "We have several butchers in the area that slaughter and package for farmers. I figure I can advertise the birds for sale and provide a list of the butchers for anyone wishing to have the birds dressed and shipped overnight."

The dryer buzzed and Mackie went to get the clothes and brought them back to fold and talk with the weary Eric. "I thought about raising all kinds of domestic exotic birds but when I heard the racket that peacocks made I decided against it." When she had all the clothing folded she looked toward Eric and saw that he had fallen asleep while she talked. *I must have talked him to sleep*. His driver's license said he was twenty-five years old but right now he looked like a battered homeless teenager in her loaner clothes and the afghan around his shoulders. That train of thought brought up too many buried memories so she turned off all the lights except the one over the kitchen sink, and went to bed.

Mackie woke up to the sound of thunder overhead, No, *wait, that's not thunder, what the hell?* She noticed the time and seen she had slept for four hours. It was eight a.m. She ran into the living room and saw that Eric must have woken up sometime during the night and taken the clothing into the bedroom with him. She knocked on the bedroom door with a quiet tap, "Hey, guys, I think we have company." The murmured "be right out" was answer enough for her as she made her way into the kitchen and the coffee pot. She could still hear the steady whap whap of the helicopter blades over the house and knew it was a matter of time before someone would be knocking on her door. Until Eric emerged from the bedroom she wouldn't know if the visitors were friendly or not so she reached into the top cupboard and pulled down the solid plastic box. She knew Eric was at the kitchen door as she loaded the Smith and Wesson with a full clip and jacked a shell into the chamber.

"I think it's my family, Mackie, you won't need that." Eric was dressed and sat down to put his shoes on. "I hit my panic button last night and they would have tracked me here." When he went to the door she handed him the pistol. He took the gun from her, mostly to calm her fears for his safety. He knew his grandfather would have sent the chopper for him as soon as the emergency alarm had reached the family security offices. This entire week had been fucked up so why would he expect their rescue to be anything less than a circus. He watched as the chopper sat down in the only spot that was clear enough for it to land. Five men piled out of the side the minute it sat level. One man followed them and he knew Granddad had sent Uncle Liam to retrieve him. He put the gun in the back of his waistband and walked toward the advancing men.

Chapter 2

When the men surrounded Eric, he told them, "I'm fine, the SUV is toast, and I do mean toast. The truck is across the driveway in those woods. I got lucky, just a knock on the head and some scrapes." Everyone but Liam took off to see the wrecked vehicle, and he dreaded the coming discussion with his uncle. No one knew he was in the area and he had neglected to leave his destination with the family when he left the house on Tuesday. His father was in Europe dealing with some company emergency there, so he knew Liam would be on the rescue mission to retrieve him. When the family found out about Jenny and EJ he was really going to catch hell.

By the look on his uncle's face, Liam was pissed off at his carelessness. He knew then he was in deep shit. When he got close enough to talk he started to hold out his hand to shake Liam's, but the man was already grabbing his shirt and drawing back to punch him. The sound of a gunshot and the dirt kicking up the mud near the big man's left foot stopped the fist as both men turned toward the woman who had followed Eric outside.

"Let him go or I take out your arm at the shoulder Mr." When the big man didn't release his grip on Eric's shirt, she said, "This is a Colt .45 with hollow point bullets, do you really think you can hit him before my next bullet takes your shoulder out? I said let him go."

Eric started to turn to tell her that it was okay when another shot rang out, dropping the woman where she stood. The two men watched the surprise on her face as her eyes closed and she melted to the ground. Eric started screaming at the shooter as he ran to Mackie.

"*You stupid sonofabitch*. She was protecting me you dumbfuck." He knelt in the mud next to her and saw the hole in her upper chest. The bullet had gone through her chest and looked to be lodged in her right arm. The arm she was using to point the gun at Liam. As shots went it was a good one, though unfortunately for Mackie. He pulled the shirt away from the wound and saw the bloody mess of ragged flesh and blood. "Dammit, somebody help me here, she is losing too damn much blood." He pulled his shirt off and pressed the material to the open wound and kept telling her it would be okay, they would get her to the hospital and find a doctor to patch her up. "Hang in there, Mackie, I'll get you some help." He looked around and saw three men and not one of them had moved since Mackie dropped to the ground so he tried to pick her up himself but couldn't budge her deadweight. "We need to load her in the chopper and get her to a hospital, Uncle, because if we don't get her some help you might as well get ready to go to prison for murder."

Mackie could hear men's voices and she felt herself being carried. There was pain in her shoulder and she started to fight the strong arms that were holding her so tightly, but the man's strength kept her in his embrace and she could hear another man telling her she would be okay. She felt a needle go into her arm and knew she was being drugged into sleep.

When Jenny saw them bringing Mackie back to the house bleeding, surrounded by all the huge men, she started to shake. She saw Eric without his shirt and could only stare at him for a minute before hobbling across the room into his arms and crying that she wanted to go home. "Please, Eric, just take me and the baby back to my place and we will be fine, just let me go back, please." Her face was swollen on the right side and she was limping and holding her wrist close to her body where Mackie had fashioned a sling for her to hold it. Her hair was matted from going to sleep with wet hair and she was a bedraggled mess but she had never looked more beautiful to the man who held her.

"Uncle, I would like to introduce you to your new niece, Jenny, and in case you missed what she said, we have a son, Eric Junior." As if the baby heard his name being said he started to whimper and Jenny let go of her husband to see to the little one.

Liam gave Eric a hard look and followed the tiny female into the bedroom to see for himself what kind of trouble the kid had gotten himself into this time. He saw Jenny pull her swollen wrist from the sling and try to pick the baby up with both hands. She ended up rolling the child from the baby seat and into her injured arm, she must not have noticed him standing there watching her because she used her good hand to pull up her blouse and bare her breast for the baby to suckle. The sight of the tiny woman nourishing the small infant was good enough for Liam, at least she loved the child and probably loved his nephew too if what he seen in the kitchen was any indication of her feelings. She seemed very young and Liam wondered where Eric had found her.

John Fielding was taking care of Mackie. He was a doctor, and one of Liam's closest friends, and it was a good thing he had been there today. His normal job was in the research and development department of Klinger International's medical division. He liked going on field trips with the guys occasionally but this one wasn't turning out quite as good as he had hoped. The woman had lost quite a bit of blood. She also had some history with violence from the numerous scars he saw while working to staunch the blood and secure the wound. The deep scratches on her hips were a mystery but the cuts on her hands and arms supported the story that Eric was relating about the rescue. From what Fielding had seen of the wreckage, he could believe she sustained them while rescuing the family. A bloody miracle the SUV hadn't blown up instead of just burning a little under the hood. The rain must have kept the fire from spreading.

Liam stood next to Fielding as the man sutured the exit wound closed. It looked like a small pile of hamburger before he started, now it looked like a stitched up mess of red and black lines on her white skin. The bullet that had done all the damage was still lodged in her arm just above the wrist and Fielding had him hold her arm so he could remove it. Luckily it hadn't severed the artery so the blood loss was minimized but still seemed like a lot before Fielding got it stopped and the wound stitched. "We got lucky here, boss, she has a titanium plate over the bone here, it must have been a bad break at one time. The plate kept the bullet from shattering her bone. I cleaned and packed the entrance and exit wounds, and you see what I had to deal with here in front. I like this one, let's hope she doesn't hate us when she wakes up."

Since Liam had been the one to help John strip the bloody wet clothing from her body, he knew why they both looked at the woman with respect. She had several combat wounds and at least three of them looked to be bullet wounds or shrapnel and seven long thin scars from what they had assumed to be knife wounds decorating her pale body. Liam said, "She's a warrior, she'll make it. From the looks of her she has seen a lot worse than this. Damn woman, she thought I was going to harm Eric. She had to have seen the team with their rifles before she pulled that .45 on me for Christ's sakes." When Liam thought about the deadly look on the woman's face as she threatened to shoot him, he believed she would have done just what she threatened to do if she hadn't been shot first or he hadn't let go of his nephew.

Fielding left to go check on Jenny and Eric. They still had unattended wounds and various ailments that needed a doctor's opinion.

Liam sat with Mackie, from the driver's license he found while rummaging through her purse he knew her name was Maxine Vaught and she was thirty years old. Her height was five feet ten inches and she weighed one hundred seventy-five pounds, her eye color was blue and she had brown hair. Those were all statistics from the State of Michigan but he knew more. She had the heart of a lioness when it came to protecting those who she claimed. She was also reckless but beautifully put together. He knew what those big breasts looked like and how a man would lose himself in those tender pillows with the delightful cherry red tips. Her hips flared wide and were just the correct size for a man's hands to hold while sinking deep inside of her warmth. He decided she would be theirs, if her true personality matched her skills as a potential lady friend. He only hoped she would be open to the notion.

She was semi-conscious by the time the men walked out of her room, and through the slit of her eyes she could plainly see his face again. There was no mistake. The man was the same one who had caught her eyes twice in the past few years when she was in Detroit. She often wondered about him, and truthfully the two men she'd seen him with at those times, but hadn't had time to learn who they were. Now he was in her home, and she'd threatened to shoot him. Handsome or not, sexy or not, she would have shot him, and apologized after the fact. As it was, she'd been so shocked to see him standing there ready to punch Eric, she hesitated with her first shot and that was not like her. The burning pain in her shoulder and arm was dulled, but not gone, and she let the pain pull her under in sleep. She knew it would get worse before too long, and she would get no sleep from the unrelenting nerves and tissue damage.

Liam had the phone on speaker in a conference call between his grandfather and his father. Eric sat next to him and Jenny sat next to Eric with the little guy on her lap. She held him with her left arm and looked comfortable as she sat quietly. "I've had the SUV towed and it is on its way to you for our people to inspect. Eric and Jenny and the baby are fine but as I told you the woman is still not able to stay alone. Any suggestions?" As they talked, a large grey cat jumped onto the table and plopped its butt in front of Liam. The cat started batting at the golden chain around Liam's neck that was hanging loosely and dangling while the man rested his forearms on the table.

The baby was awake and started to fuss and the, "What is that noise? Are you talking about a *REAL BABY*"? The question was asked by Eric's great granddad who was Liam's grandfather, Mason Klinger. Jenny cringed back at the harshness of his voice and Eric confirmed that, "Yes, Granddad, it is a real baby, my baby, and my wife's name is Jennifer. I think you will like them both. I can hardly wait for dad to get back from overseas, he's going to love her too." He gave Jenny a reassuring smile before picking up little Eric and taking Jenny's arm to lead them into the bedroom to change EJ, as Eric had started to call his son.

Liam glared at the young man as he left him sitting there to answer the older men's questions. "We can go into more detail after we sort this out here. Long story short is that Eric's car was shot at and forced off the road with his wife and infant son in it, the woman who is laying in the next room dragged them all out of the vehicle at great peril to herself and brought them into her home, and patched them up as best she could. When we arrived it spooked her, and I was too busy getting ready to punch out Eric's lights for scaring me half to death when she sent a round into the ground as a warning and threatened to shoot me if I hurt him. Tracey saw someone with a gun pointed my way and shot her. That's why we are still here, it's not like I can just leave a woman who saved Eric's life and got shot by our people to her own devices. We will be lucky if she doesn't sue us as it sits right now."

Liam said his goodbyes and hung up the connection. He called the team in and told them his plans. "Tracey, Jordon, and Mortimer will ride back with Eric and his family in the chopper. Fielding and Reynolds will stay here with me until you send the chopper back tomorrow. According to the weather report it's going to sleet all night tonight and the wind is supposed to be gusting at thirty-five mph. We'll be fine here for another day or two if we need to stay longer."

Liam had to swear on his mother's heart that he would make sure Mackie got through the next few days, and that Liam wouldn't yell at her or upset her in any way when she woke up before Eric would step a foot outside of the door.

"You don't understand, Uncle, it's not just because she got hurt on my behalf, she saved Jenny and EJ and came back to save me too. It's more a debt of honor as Granddad would say." Eric grabbed Jenny's purse and the diaper bag in his free hand, the other arm was holding the child's safety seat with the handsome baby sleeping comfortably. Jenny was being carried to the helicopter. "Uncle, I can't tell you how important Mackie is to Jenny and I, think of it as if it was you that she crawled through broken glass and risked her life for. What's her life worth to you after you're safe?"

When the chopper took off Liam went into the bedroom to check on Mackie. She was obviously in pain but not one sound came from her. Her back was arched and sweat beaded her forehead and her teeth were bared and clenched. He looked at her hands and found them fisted and trembling.

"Fielding. Fielding, get in here!" he shouted.

Turning to Mackie, he said, "Come on, honey, I'm getting help, hang in there."

"Fielding, where are you?" and then he ran into the bathroom to get a cold towel to try to cool her down. By the time Fielding came rushing into the room Liam had her stripped to the waist and cold towels almost covering her head and torso. The doctor brought his medical kit in the room with him and prepared a shot of antibiotics and one for pain.

"Damn, I was afraid of this happening, all I have is Demerol for pain and I hope she isn't allergic. I used the last of the lightweight stuff when I sewed her up. I wasn't anticipating having to do surgery on a woman when we left Detroit." He shot the needle into her arm and helped Liam pull her into a sitting position to run the cool towel over her back as soon as she went limp. "I'll be damned, how in the hell did I miss those?" He was referring to the mass of scars on her back that could have only come from being whipped with something meant to cause pain. "What the hell was this woman into that would cause all these scars?"

After Fielding checked and redressed her wounds, he set up a makeshift IV to get some much needed fluid into her body. He went to make a pot of coffee because it might be a long damn night if she became feverish again. Liam stayed by her side willing the woman to tell him her secrets. No woman that he had ever seen had been through what this one had. It appeared the only places not riddled with scars were her face and from the top of her breasts up to her neck. He felt no pity for her, just rage at those who had hurt her so badly. He started searching her room for clues about her life. The pictures hanging on the walls all featured animals. Her drawers contained serviceable jeans, t-shirts, and cotton underwear. He found himself disappointed there wasn't a thong in the bunch. The sexiest thing in her wardrobe was an expensive skirt and blazer set from a chain store. He noted three pairs of shoes and wasn't really surprised to find a gun safe hidden in the closet.

Fielding came in two hours later to allow Liam to check on his messages and grab a bite to eat. As he sat next to her on the bed, he studied her body and the scars decorating so many inches of her tall frame. "I wonder if your personality matches up with the hell you've been through." He brushed the hair from her cheek, and bent to give her lips a light peck, but when he felt her breath whisper over his lips, he rested his forehead to hers. He decided then and there that he would do his best to find out and reconnect with her as soon as she was in better health. She fascinated him, and the fact made him shake his head. "Such strength, and unless I miss my guess, that strength is why you appear to be so alone here in the middle of nowhere, with a cat, and enough guts to shoot a stranger over another stranger." He pulled the sheet up over her naked body, and left the room before he gave into the impulse to lay down next to her in an effort to comfort her.

Liam fed the cat and continued his search for information about the homeowner. He found nothing until he pulled a laptop from her desk drawer and opened it. The thing was password protected but he cracked it within an hour, FOUR CATZ opened the screen, and he set about snooping through all the information from the computer that he could get into. However, several files he came across he couldn't gain access to, so he shut down the system and put the laptop back where he found it.

Darryl supervised the loading of Eric's SUV, and watched as the flatbed drove away before heading back to the little house. He wanted to see if the avenging angel was awake. She was the kind of woman he liked to look at. Her actions so far just made him want to know more about her. He pulled out his phone and sent an e-mail to his office. Eric said her name was Maxine Vaught, aka Mackie. Ham and

Gribbler would know what he wanted, and they'd be thorough.

Once the men gathered in the small kitchen, they discussed the woman in the next room.

"She has a small fortune in guns and at least one in every room." The Smith and Wesson she loaned Eric was sitting on the kitchen counter, the 1911 Colt was sitting beside it and he had counted two loaded 12 gauge pump shotguns over the front and back doors. "There are more pistols under the bathroom sink, next to her bed, and one in the cupboard filled with glasses in the kitchen. She's either paranoid or she has some pretty impressive enemies." Liam decided to call his father back. If anyone could find out about anything or anyone, it was Drummond Klinger.

Darryl listened to the two people in the world that meant the most to him, and added his opinion to the conversation. "I like her, Tyler was doing his job, but I wanted to drop the fucker where he stood when I saw her fall." His hands rose and fell. "One minute she stood there with that gun in her hand and, yeah, all of that hair blowing around. I saw her and wanted to come back to talk, but she dropped and, let's just say it was a good thing that driveway is a couple of hundred feet deep. I had time to cool off before I reached you." He got up and walked into the bedroom to reassure himself that she was still breathing.

Chapter 3

Mackie was resting quietly, and the men were watching Monday Night football, when a distinctive click was heard throughout the house. They watched as the windows were covered with metal panels sliding from the side walls and they could hear the outer doors lock down. A small red light was blinking near the television until Darryl Reynolds who was closest to the television looked, and punched the button with his finger like it might bite him. The TV went blank for a moment and the screen displayed four different views of the perimeter of the house and yard. The infrared cameras had excellent contrast and the three men watched the screen to see what had triggered the house into button down mode.

The bushes were moving, at least that is what it looked like, but every man in the room knew what those bushes were. More men stepped out of the trees and Liam counted five men and four Bushmen approaching the house. He noted that every man carried assault rifles and full combat belts.

"Shit," the three men looked toward Mackie standing in the doorway of her bedroom pulling on a sweater over her wounded arm and shoulder. Her eyes were on the screen but she spoke slowly and quietly to them. "I would appreciate it if you guys would gather the guns

I am sure you have found by now, and bring them into my bedroom." When no one moved, she looked toward them and said, "I'm not going to be able to protect you unless you do as I say." Her body was swaying slightly and Liam stood, Mackie held up her good hand, "Look, I can get us to safety if you will co-operate and do as I ask you to do. Now grab my guns please and come into my bedroom." She made a kissy noise and the grey cat ran to her as she turned back into her room.

Reynolds and Fielding looked to Liam to set the plan. He nodded and went to the kitchen and grabbed the four pistols he knew were there, and the shotgun from over the door. Fielding had the pistol from the bathroom and the shotgun from the front door and Reynolds helped Liam carry his cache as they filed into her small bedroom. She pushed Reynolds and Liam into her closet with the cat and tried to smile. "There is a button when you get to the basement on the right side. The room directly on the right at the hall across from the elevator is where we'll meet you. Please send the lift back up." She slapped the wall next to the closet door and the floor moved downwards taking a pissed Liam and an amazed Reynolds with it.

Mackie looked at Fielding and told him to stay put. But he followed her because she looked like she was going to collapse at any minute. She wobbled into the kitchen and opened the cupboard next to the back door, and she flipped a toggle switch and then made her way into the living room, and armed the explosives there too. Fielding watched the TV screen for a few seconds while she was stumbling over the furniture and he saw something to make his blood run cold. A long dark colored SUV was backed up about twenty yards from the house and the back doors were opened to reveal a 50 caliber machine gun mounted in the back. "Fuck, com' on we need to get out of here." And he tried to get a grip on her good arm, but Mackie was heading to the bedroom before he could grab her and he followed. The lift was back in place by the time they got back into the closet and she slapped the wall again to send them down to join the others.

The ride down seemed to last forever and for a short while they could hear gunfire above their heads, but all was quiet now. When the lift finally stopped at the bottom, Mackie straightened up from her slouched lean on the wall and exited the box, and slowly made her way down the corridor with Fielding trailing behind her. She turned left then went twenty feet more and turned right. They walked to a door that was heavy, "Okay, He-Man, you want to open this heavy assed door for the damsel in distress please?" Fielding opened the door and they walked inside the cozy room.

It looked like a rec room complete with a pool table and a bar in the corner. Mackie went right to the entertainment center and picked up the remote that Liam had just put down because he couldn't get the damn thing to work. She twisted it, clicked the button, and the TV came on. Once again they watched as the small army shot at the doors and windows of the little house. When one genius tried to pry a window panel away from the opening after he broke out the glass the ground exploded under his feet. His body flew up in the air and landed in pieces almost out of camera range. The same thing happened in the front of the house to a brave soul. His body did fly out of camera range. "Okay, guys, here's the deal, tell me how much damage happens when they hit my house with that 50 caliber if I pass out before it happens, stay in this room until I wake up again and I'll see about getting you home safe."

Mackie was asleep when the big gun opened fire on her little house. Unfortunately for the attackers, the entire house and yard lit up like the fourth of July, complete with the rocket's red glare. The three men stared at the screen long minutes after the last detonation had gone off. The SUV was toast and so were the occupants. The men standing farther back to let the 50 cal do its work had danced around jerking and twitching until they dropped to the ground. The cameras were still on and Liam tried to count the bodies of the fallen men. He came up with ten on the ground and felt damn glad he hadn't been in the house when it blew apart. It appeared that no one had escaped the devastation within the scope of the camera lenses.

Reynolds whistled as he watched the screen scanning for any signs of life. He looked at Mackie's innocent sleeping face. "I don't know about you guys, but I sure want to know who this little gal is. She's done pissed off somebody who wants her ass dead. She knew and planned for every eventuality, I don't know what happened to those guys there," he said as he pointed to the bodies laying on the farthest perimeters on the screen. "It looks like they were dancing on electricity running into them from the ground, look at their boots." Liam and Fielding looked at what Reynolds was talking about. It appeared the boots were melted on the men's feet. Although the picture was clear for infrared you would still have a hard time making out details clearly.

Liam sat back in the chair directly across from where Mackie lay sleeping. He knew the undeserved resentment for her taking charge while she was so injured was dumb, but his ego was taking a beating around this woman. She was obviously in the security business, whether she was still at it or retired from it, he had yet to learn. Her knowledge of weapons rivaled Reynolds and he was a twenty year Veteran with the Navy, fifteen of those years had been with the SEALs. She must be something if she impressed Darryl Reynolds. The man had damn near as many scars as she did. His came from almost being blown to hell by an IED in Iraq. Hers came from years of injuries. The whip marks on her back could have come from an overzealous sadistic lover but Liam doubted that. Even a sadist would hesitate to mark a lover that severely.

If she was in security the gunshot wounds could be explained, but the knife wounds? The various other scars? No, there was a story here and he hoped to find out what it was sooner than later. Fielding told him that her previous injuries were mostly old ones. The whip marks on her back Fielding thought she must have gotten as a child for the scars to have healed and became so faded. The rest were more recent.

Mackie knew she was being watched, she allowed her eyelids to rise only wide enough to see the man sitting opposite from where she was lying. Her mind identified his face as the man she planned to shoot if he hurt Eric, and she must have been shot because the rest was a bit fuzzy in her mind. She remembered men's voices and pain in her shoulder and right wrist. Telling herself to get her lazy ass up was easy, actually moving was the hard part. *I'm going to have to start exercising again,* she promised her sore muscles.

"I am assuming that you are either the one who shot me or the one responsible for getting me shot?" Mackie started talking before she moved. As she sat up, she said, "Let's also assume that Eric and Jenny got away before the shit hit the fan around here." She pushed the hair off her face and really looked at the man in front of her. Tall, maybe six four, two twenty, dark reddish brown hair, and dark blue eyes with wide shoulders and grim faced. "Sorry we haven't been introduced, I am Maxine Vaught. I would shake your hand but as we can see I am kind of tied up here at the moment." She was referring to the sling holding her arm up and secured in place with a thick strip of gauze wrapped around her ribs.

Reynolds and Fielding stopped their game of pool when she started talking and came to sit with Liam and Mackie. "I am Liam Klinger, on my right is Doctor John Fielding, and to my left is Darryl Reynolds, head of security for Klinger International." When she acknowledged the men with a nod to each, he continued, "Yes, my nephew and his family left this morning in the chopper with the other three men that came with me, including the man who shot you, I didn't want you to possibly retaliate against him for doing his job, which is to protect me and my family."

He waited for her to speak, but his impatience got the better of him. "I believe that as guests of your house we are entitled to an explanation of last night's impromptu deadly entertainment if you please." His companions nodded their heads as he finished speaking. He waited in vain, her head was shaking slowly sideways. "Ms. Vaught, I assure you that we are not the helpless desk jockeys you believe us to be. In spite of our allowing you to take charge in the emergency situation, it's not our way to hide behind an injured woman." Her head straightened when he said the "allow her" statement. "I am not trying to insult you or your abilities, merely telling you that we are normally competent men in an emergency. This has been a complete clusterfuck from our point of view since my nephew had his unfortunate run-in with a jealous co-worker."

Mackie had to laugh a bit, and that arched his brow. *Looks like I not only bruised his ego, I also insulted his speech.* "I'm afraid that you are going to be disappointed, since I have no idea what you're talking about. And after some starched up guy with *pretty ribbons and shiny stars* has a talk with you, I won't be the only one who has no clue as to what might have or might not have happened here." She had given them as much information as she dared, even if she did think they deserved some kind of explanation. It wasn't her call. Smiling at the sexy trio of men, Mackie offered a bit of advice. "If it were me? I would try to think of last night as one of your nephew's virtual video games and you pressed the right buttons to kick some bad guy's ass."

Liam watched her disappear into the bathroom and wanted to demand that she tell him what kind of trouble they were facing last night. He was smart enough to pick up on the shiny stars comment, so at least she had given them that much. Still, watching her ass sway across ten feet of floor after seeing her completely nude just hours ago brought his brain back to his earlier carnal thoughts concerning just how good it would be to hold that ass in his hands while his cock was buried inside of her body. *I must be out of my tiny mind.*

Mackie took one look at her image in the bathroom mirror and wanted to screech at the sight. Her long brown hair was a rat's nest and when she tried to pull her fingers through it she dislodged a few pieces of dead grass and leaves. She had a new scrape on her cheek to go with her newest bullet wounds and until she did a complete assessment of damages, she wouldn't know what other injuries she might have sustained in the past forty-eight hours. She stripped off her clothes and looked to the shoulder wound. Damn, that was going to leave a starfish scar. Four inches to the left and down two inches and she wouldn't be bitching about another scar, she wouldn't be bitching about anything ever again.

She rummaged around in the cabinet and found the transparent adhesive tape that would keep the wounds from getting wet while she took a shower. She lathered her hair and while it took longer to rinse out with only one hand, the hot water helped sooth her sore muscles. Her thoughts turned to the attack last night. She was warned there was a leak somewhere pretty high up and now they had proof sitting right outside her door. It was a good thing she planned to rebuild her home at some future date or she would be really upset. One thing was certain, her insurance agent would have a fit if she tried to turn that claim in.

Drying off was haphazard at best. Her hair was a problem because wrapping a towel around the long strands of wet hair kept escaping her efforts. Finally in frustration she just rubbed the messy wet mass as dry as she could and let it go. Mackie grabbed a set of sweats out of the cabinet and pulled them on. She wished she had a bra to wear but since none was with her other clothing she didn't worry about it. With the wound being right where a bra strap would sit, a bra would be out of the question anyway. No panties were available either but that wasn't a big deal. The knock on the bathroom door startled her.

She heard Reynolds call out to her, "Ma'am, you might want to come out here and see this." She didn't hesitate to open the door and head to the adjoining room. Reynolds caught her before she collided with his hard body. "Calm down, sugar, there's time, Liam noticed that someone was out there doing recon. We wondered if this is one of the good guys and thought you might know."

Mackie hurried over to the monitor and pulled out a keyboard from the wooden frame of the entertainment center. Fielding and Reynolds looked at each other with surprise. They had gone over every inch of the room and had overlooked that. Each man wondered what else he might have missed. The woman had more gadgets than most action movies and Reynolds found himself envious of the toys she was so comfortable commanding.

Liam watched her fingers fly over the keyboard and wondered what she was doing this time. "Are you going to blow up another building?" She ignored his sarcastic question, and he was not a man who was used to being ignored. He kept goading her, trying to get her to talk to him, to let him in on what she was doing this time. "Ms. Vaught, I'm afraid I will have to demand answers, the company helicopter will be flying back sometime this morning to pick us up, and when they see what your house looks like now, they will certainly dispatch the authorities out here." Maybe his veiled threat of sending outside influences in would rattle her, but all it did was earn him a quick side glance from her blue eyes.

It didn't help his mood when first Darryl gave him a hard glare, and then John told him to stop acting like a royal prick while they watched her in action. He'd come close and leaned over to whisper near Liam's ear.

"You can stop acting like Lord Klinger at anytime now. She's doing her job and you know it, just because she hasn't got a cock growing between her legs, doesn't give you permission to act like a sonofabitch." John had shaken his head and walked away from him with a disgusted look on his face.

Mackie watched the two men filtering through the rubble of what was left of her home. She used a small toggle on the keyboard to maneuver the cameras to check the perimeter more closely. If there were more men out there she wanted to know about it. The picture zoomed in on one of the men's faces and the men beside her heard her curse. "That miserable fucking bastard, I've got you now you sonofabitch." She kept the camera on her prey as her left hand continued to type into the keyboard. She started talking to her companions without pause in watching the screen or typing.

"Gentlemen, you see the man on this screen? He is a man about to be charged with treason if the people coming to arrest him get to him before he steps on one of the undetonated explosive devices buried around the property." She pointed to the second man who stood back from the wreckage watching for anything to move. His gun was drawn down in position to spray bullets into anything that might spook him or his partner. "That man better hope he stays right where he is because about two and a half feet to his right is something that will literally light up his life." She looked away from the monitor to make eye contact with the men that were watching her rather than the screen. "If you are squeamish or are prone to get sick watching a man blow himself up, you might want to turn your head or find something else to do for a while. It will be another five minutes or so before help arrives and I refuse to disarm anything until they do get here."

Chapter 4

Mackie watched as Reynolds rubbed his hands together and squatted down in front of the monitor watching the slow moving man picking his way through the rubble. She grinned and shook her head, *obviously military and certainly Special Ops or one of the Black Ops boys*, she thought. She watched as Fielding went to the fridge and grabbed a can of soda. Certainly a doctor wouldn't want to watch needless death. It surprised her that Fielding came back and sat next to her to watch what might happen next. Liam sat quietly on her other side and Mackie was beginning to feel like the meat in a sandwich. Neither man touched her but she felt their warmth and it made her wish for things she couldn't have. *They would probably freak out if she suggested they all get naked and snuggle together.*

It had been a long time since she had been intimate with a man. Years in fact, before she joined the agency, before she got all the scars decorating her skin now. The long thin lines on her back were gifts from the slavers. At the age of ten she had been abducted and used as a slave by a drug selling gang, along with six other children, to package their poison white powder. Mackie and the rest of the children learned to keep their heads down and their hands busy to avoid being whipped. Unfortunately, she had been born a protector and had gotten beatings many times for interfering with another child's punishment. She was one of the three children who were saved during a bloody turf war. The gang's rivals showed up one day and opened fire on the gang that held her and the other children.

When they heard the gunfire, the three girls had huddled together in the dingy room in a corner until the shooting stopped and no further noise could be heard. It seemed like hours before she got up and opened the door to see what had happened. The seven people in the next room were in various positions around the tables and chairs, they had been killed before they understood what was going on. Mackie watched as Renaldo limped around the room gathering as much money as he could carry in his plastic grocery bag. She thought it strange at the time that he never looked back when he slowly opened the door and cautiously peeked around it to check and see if the rivals had left the area before slipping outside.

Mackie had turned fifteen by then. Her companions, Carmen and Flora, were fourteen-year-old twins. The girls had cautiously gathered the messy stacks of twenties and hundred dollar bills and filled a backpack for each of them. Carmen and Flora wanted to go home to their family and, after the girls found clean clothing in a closet where their keepers had slept, they slipped out of the building. Mackie went with them to the bus station and watched as they boarded the bus to take them back to San Antonio. Mackie had no home to go to. Her parents were a distant memory. She had been taken from a foster home in Tulsa, Oklahoma.

After leaving the bus station, Mackie decided to go back to the small dingy house and wait until morning to decide what she was going to do. Her back was still bloody from the whipping that Carlos enjoyed giving her almost daily now. She left the bodies where they laid and started going through several envelopes of papers. Some looked like deeds to land, some were I.O.U's from the junkies and dope peddlers that visited the little house each time a new batch of drugs were delivered. She gathered the things she thought were deeds and the rest of the larger denomination bills. By the time she was ready to leave, she had to figure out how to carry the three heavy black totes full of cash and papers. She didn't know how to drive so taking one of the many vehicles in the driveway wasn't an option, she searched the house looking for inspiration and found a large suitcase with a handle and wheels to transfer the heavy cache into so she was left with a large suitcase and a messenger bag.

She left the only home she had known for years that afternoon taking Bianca's state identification with her. Bianca had been one of the slave children until Jorge decided that she would make a good bed companion and took her into his room. Within a few weeks Bianca was an addict. She always sported bruises on her limbs and face but the white powder made the pain go away. She remembered the way Jorge would make Bianca crawl on her hands and knees to beg for the white poison. First he would tell her to lick his cock and he would sprinkle the powder over the surface of his damp flesh and tell her to pull the cheeks of her ass wide for her reward. He would slam his hard cock into her cunt or asshole, whichever slot his thick cock hit first, and she would scream and beg him for more as he brutally forced himself inside of her body. Two days before, she watched as he gave her to two of his friends as she begged for the drug and one man laid down forcing her to straddle his small cock while the other shoved his into her rear hole. Jorge shoved his cock into her mouth, pulled it out, and dipped it into a small plastic tub of the powder, coating his thick cock from head to pubic hair. Bianca swallowed his cock down her throat and her body went wild.

The men slapped her all over her body and Jorge yanked her hair back and forth while choking her on his hardness. When the three men had finished, Bianca offered herself to every man in the room. When Jorge pulled her into the bathroom, Mackie could hear the water flowing from the shower and Bianca kept begging for more. Jorge dragged her back into the room and pushed her down onto the table. He spread her legs and took a straw that he filled with the powder before inserting it into Bianca's cunt. He blew the powder into her passage and sat down between her legs. He shoved her knees up to her naked breasts and pinched her nipples cruelly while his hands were there, his fingers pulled the hairy lips of her pussy apart and his mouth covered her hole. He sucked and tongued her as her body shook. When he had gotten all of the cocaine laced juice from her cunt that he could, he stood over her and pushed his fingers into her cunt.

He laughed as she squealed and Renaldo took the opportunity to push his hard cock into her mouth as he grabbed her hair then shoved her head down further onto his length, he allowed her to breathe and shoved her head back, time after time, while Jorge worked his entire hand into her abused pussy. The men finally tired of their game and after showering Bianca with their sperm left her lying there on the table playing with her own nipples and singing a nursery rhyme. Before Mackie left the house, she covered Bianca with a sheet and said a clumsy prayer to a God that had no meaning for her.

Mackie wondered still now how she had survived those first two weeks at a rundown no tell motel in Houston, Texas. If she hadn't met Louisa Vaught, it probably wouldn't have gone nearly as well. The woman was homeless. She worked as a maid at the hotel, when a room became empty she would clean the room and put clean sheets on the bed. One day when she was leaving the building, Mackie had a brilliant idea. Louisa was older than she was and Mackie had enough money and deeds to seven properties. She invited the woman into her room and after an hour of not so subtle questioning, Louisa had point blank asked Mackie what this was all about. A week later Louisa Vaught and her younger sister, Maxine, moved into a modest home in one of the nicer neighborhoods of Reno, Nevada.

Mackie then thought about the bullet wounds and knife wounds from the many missions she was sent on in the past ten years. Who needs tattoos when her skin was decorated by so many pink scars in varying stages of the color. Being tortured for information about classified documents with a box cutter almost broke her. She knew the long thin scars would be with her for the rest of her life. Her torturers had left her for dead not realizing that none of the slices were deep enough to kill her even if they did bleed like crazy. Mackie hadn't felt the slices at first until one creative bastard slapped her and poured a bottle of whiskey over the wounds and laughed while she screamed.

The three bullet wound scars were from a drive-by assassination attempt on a United States Senator visiting Iraq. Mackie had the misfortune to be the first agent to step out of a building and the overanxious shooter thought she was the Senator and opened fire before Senator Downs walked out of the door. The Senator was fine, the wounds ended Mackie's career as a bodyguard for high profile politicians. When she finally healed enough to be discharged from the hospital in Germany and came back to the States, she decided to keep protecting people, just doing it now on a different scale and in a more covert way. This little plot of land had been home for two years now and she loved the place. It had been perfect for her new enterprise since the old nuke bunker was buried deep underground. The little house that she felt so at home in was gone now. And although Mackie knew she had plans to rebuild, she wondered if the site was completely compromised.

Mackie knew that at least two of these guys had seen her naked and wondered why neither man asked about the scars. *They probably were raised with manners and know better than to bring up something so personal, you dingy.* She wouldn't give them an explanation anyway.

Reynolds' whoop brought her back to the present and she saw what had aroused his interest. Her fingers quickly flew over the keyboard disarming the detonation devices to prevent the probability of an American soldier's death. The solders came from the woods and a large helicopter landed in the same area that the Klinger Corporation chopper was sitting yesterday. The sleet was making it harder to see what was happening but they did see both men who had been picking through the wreckage chased down and cuffed by several men in olive drab.

The dead bodies were photographed and slid into body bags stacked side by side next to the helicopter's wide open cargo doors. Body parts were placed into plastic bins and stacked with the whole bodies. Two large trucks towing trailers pulled into sight and Mackie groaned," they're putting ruts in my driveway." Within three hours the site where her home had been was cleared dirt. The burned out SUV was loaded on the trailers and curtained sides raised to keep curious onlookers from seeing what was on the trailer bed, the blackened pieces of her home were in the back dump box. Twelve bodies plus two large plastic boxes filled with body parts were loaded into the chopper and the prisoners were shackled in the back of the cargo hold. The sleet had stopped so the chopper had no problems lifting and flying off as the trucks and personnel transport left.

Reynolds was talking to the screen as he watched the efficiency of the soldiers. "That's right, boys, don't forget to look around the perimeter for all them body parts, you don't want some hunter finding a piece of leg or a few fingers." He pointed to the screen like he might be directing the searchers for any leftover evidence. "Those soldiers are just lucky it is so damn cold or the smell of the dead would be making more than a couple of those boys lose their breakfast."

As she waited for General Thomas Hurrell to travel to the bunker, she held herself upright by holding on to the various pieces of furniture until she reached the far wall. She stood for a moment, resting her tired body on the wall, and gathered her energy to step back far enough to pull the framed picture of cats aside. She punched in more numbers and waited for the light to glow blue, before waving her hand to the men for them to join her. The wall opened by sliding into itself, like pocket doors. On the other side was a barracks with three sets of bunk beds.

"I'm sorry I can't offer you better accommodations, but this is as good as I have. You can get some sleep, and someone will be here by morning to make sure you get home safely." She turned and eyed the distance to the couch, before swaying to the comfortable space. She didn't lie down as much as she fell down onto the cushions. She was asleep before Fielding touched her wrist to check her pulse. The cat hopped up onto the back of the couch and hissed at him when he tried to move her into a more comfortable position. "Oh for crying out loud, cat, I'm not hurting her, she needs to be moved onto her back and propped up in case she… What the fuck, now I'm talking to a damn cat." He shook his head and looked back to Liam, "Hey, bossman, I need some help here."

They ended up moving her to the end of the sectional where they'd discovered it had a reclining feature earlier while watching football. Fielding was checking the bandaging job she'd done before her shower and saw the wet mess of her wounds. The clear bandage was not meant for injuries such as hers, so he found her cache of medical supplies in the bathroom cupboard and re-bandaged her wounds. His medical pack was still lying by the door and Liam handed it to him so he could give her another shot of the antibiotics and the last of the pain meds. "I'm relatively sure she won't get up and run around again this time. Her body is in safe mode. I've seen men our size do the same thing she just did after they'd been given enough pain medication to put a normal person in a coma for at least twelve hours. When they sense danger, they're on adrenalin high. Once the danger has passed, they shut down completely. The good news is, she must feel safe. The bad news is, if she spikes another fever, we're screwed. I just gave her the last of the antibiotic I brought with me."

Liam was still struggling with his ego problem. In his family the women depended on the men, not the other way around. The sight of the woman with that gun pointed at him had also confused the hell out of him because his cock came awake in a hurry when she stood there threatening him. What she'd done made him feel as if *he* had hidden behind *her* skirts when there was danger, and that didn't settle well with him at all. Neither Fielding nor Reynolds seemed to have a problem with it. Reynolds could be excused, his ex-wife was CIA. She became an ex when she packed her shit and moved in with a fellow agent.

He must have slept for an hour or two, because the sound of the door opening and rapid footsteps could be heard coming toward his spot on the couch caused him to sit up, still half asleep. The sight of General Thomas Hurrell flanked by four others with varied ranks on their shoulders told him he was about to get his answers. His outstretched hand was ignored, as the General took a straight line to where Mackie was. The last man shook his hand and introduced himself. "How do you do, Mr. Klinger? I am Lieutenant Charles Ishmeal. I will be facilitating your trip home. If you and your men will come with me, I can get you home by lunch." The man stood there in front of him expecting his compliance with no explanation?

"It's nice to meet you, Lieutenant, but I would appreciate some sort of explanation over this. My life and that of my men has been in danger. We're whisked into a secret bunker, and are privileged to watch a real life video game, played by a woman with a fetish for guns and violence. I think we deserve some answers, don't you?"

Liam thought he had the moral high ground here. His mistake was letting his arrogance get in the way of his common sense. No one told these men what to do, unless you wore more stars than they did. He hadn't taken that into account when he'd tried to throw his importance around. These people were not boardroom minions, and the General himself let him know it.

"Mr. Klinger, on behalf of the United States of America, I apologize for any inconvenience that this ordeal has caused you. You will be receiving a formal letter of thanks in the mail to frame and put on your wall. I don't have time or the patience to deal with your curiosity right now. I need to see to Ms. Vaught and her needs before stroking your ego. Go with the Lieutenant please, before I decide to make inquiries into how our vendor got shot in the first place."

There was nothing for him to do or say. The verbal slap down was stinging his pride, but he would back off for now. Whatever rat's nest they'd stumbled into was obviously not for public consumption. He saw Fielding and Reynolds standing by the door and decided to quit before things got ugly. His father would find out what was going on. It would have to be enough for now.

"All right, General, thank you for the hospitality. I hope Ms. Vaught recovers with few lasting effects."

He turned toward the door and walked out with his men. The small electric vehicle they all piled into zipped them through pitch black tunnels with the only light coming from the headlights. Liam tried to start a conversation with the lieutenant, but the man was barely civil. His one word answers grated on Liam's nerves and it kept his temper on simmer. He had no idea where they were when they drove into daylight. They followed a path through some dense brush and stopped back at the site where Mackie's house had been. Klinger's helicopter was already waiting for them and the lieutenant pulled in close. He waited until they were in the air and drove away. Liam watched him from his seat next to the pilot, until they turned north.

Chapter 5

Thomas Hurrell, Thom to his family and close friends, was sitting by her bedside when she finally surfaced from the medically induced sleep. Her shoulder and arm felt like they were on fire, and she couldn't contain the gasp of pain that alerted him that she was awake. She was too busy trying to breathe through the pain to listen to his barking orders for the nurse to give her something to ease her suffering.

"Tell that nurse to get her ass in here with a shot for her now, the woman has been through enough for the protection of others, she shouldn't have to suffer even more." The warm feeling that his words gave her wasn't enough to stop the pain, but it allowed her to focus on him instead of her shoulder.

She wanted to ask how his wife was doing, but kept her teeth gritted to stop herself from screaming like a sissy. Screaming only got more attention and she hated it when she was the object of that attention. Especially in a hospital where everyone seemed to have access to her scars and sooner than later some well meaning person would ask her how she got them. Some called them battle tats, some drew back in revulsion, and some were fascinated in a sick way with the scars themselves. The latter ones were usually men with bent minds. Most were still in the service because they had nowhere else to go where they would find peace. They were the ones that felt they had nothing to lose, so they volunteered for the most dangerous missions that needed men with their expertise.

General Hurrell had a vested interest in her for a couple of reasons, the first was that his wife was Senator Downs, the lady that she'd been mistaken for, and was shot for the sniper's ignorance. The second and probably the most important reason was that she helped his efforts to keep important people the Government needed to hide from being discovered. Her property had an elaborate bunker deep underground, in the middle of nowhere. The place had been built back in the 1940's and once the war was over, the bunker had been forgotten.

"You can't resist, can you? The cameras picked up the way you saved those kids. Don't you ever get tired of saving people?" He waited until the nurse almost ran into the room with a capped syringe, and put the shot in her IV. Mackie's jaw slowly unclenched as the medicine began to work.

"We've had inquiries from the head of Klinger Corporation, but they are being stonewalled by Ishmeal. The old man is trying to throw his weight around, but he won't get the answers he wants, so that's one problem we don't have to concern ourselves with in the foreseeable future." He waited for her to gather

her thoughts before she would be able to converse about the situation.

"I feel like shit." Hurrell smiled at her statement. "So did you crack that traitor Edwards?"

"Oh yes, and his men decided to turn on him with the promise of one life sentence in the penitentiary instead of death. Edwards was in it for the money, he has a few very bad habits, and he planned to live in one of his choice vacation spots after the family had been killed. When they went after you, Mackie, they had no idea about the bunker. They were looking for proof to show their bankers that their mission was complete. They thought that the woman and kids were in the house with you. Edwards tried to say he was checking on you, but his timeline was screwed up and we had him dead to rights." The Diplomat's family that was being protected in the bunker was safe and the man could do his job gaining support for an alliance with America now. Neither the General nor Mackie voiced the knowledge that Edwards would never make it to trial. He would probably be found in his cell after committing suicide.

"They figured that you could be persuaded to tell them where the family was being held if they weren't at your place. When the house locked down with the steel curtains, they gave up being nice and figured you'd make a run for it. Edwards was very unappreciative of you being such a stubborn bitch. He was in a bit of pain when he confessed to planning a slow painful death for the thorn in his side for too damn long. Meaning you of course."

"Isn't that what they all seem to want to do? What is it about men that have to act like shitheads? It seems every man I've met, excluding you and Ishmeal, have the urge to compete with me to show me who wears the balls. Rich men, poor men, it doesn't matter what the walk of life, if it's testosterone based, the competition is on." She remembered Liam Klinger and his butt hurt expression when she told him that he would get his answers from someone else. She knew deep inside that men were capable of just about anything, but why did he have to act like a Neanderthal?

Thom could only repeat the same thing he always told her when she was feeling low. "Look at you, for Christ's sake, you look like a Valkyrie, carry your weight like you own it and to hell with anyone who doesn't like it. You are an attractive looking woman with an air of command, some men like to be dominated by a strong woman. The flip side is that some dominant men want to master a strong woman. The payoff is for the man who respects her strengths, and earns her respect. That man will be allowed to command her pleasure as long as she trusts him."

He grinned when the door opened and Laura Downs peeked her head through the doorway. It still surprised him when he looked at the two women in the same room, or standing together. Laura was only an inch shorter than Mackie, but their hair and eye color was the same. Laura had sprinkles of silver running through her light brown hair that was cut in a shoulder kissing length, where Mackie's hair was longer, reaching past her shoulder blades without the silver. The body style was almost identical too. His wife had hips to fit his big hands and breasts that he enjoyed at his leisure almost every night now that Laura was finishing her last term as a Senator. He hoped she wouldn't give into the pressure to run for Governor of the state. He planned to retire next year as well so they could live like normal human beings. They had a grandbaby on the way, and it was time to dangle and spoil a new generation.

Laura came up to the side of the hospital bed to check on her clone. She'd always called the woman who took bullets for her that and had never complained about it. They'd become friendly over the years and she hated seeing Mackie back in a hospital because she defended yet another person. "I see you couldn't just stay retired from the rescue business, could you?" She leaned down and brushed the younger woman's hair from her eyes where it had fallen when she tried to sit up.

Thom had to leave and make sure everything was dealt with in the matter of Edwards, but promised to see them later. He kissed his wife in a way that made Mackie envious of the closeness the two shared. Why she hadn't found such love and devotion still escaped her, but her life was all right. Lonely, but it wasn't a bad life.

Laura grinned at her once the door shut behind her still handsome loving husband. "So tell me, what did you think of Liam Klinger? He is such a dish and those two men with him, oh hell, Mackie, I think I would have locked the door and kept them as sex slaves." She waved her hand as if the thought of the men made her hot.

Mackie had to laugh, "You are going to hate me for this, my friend, but at the time, I barely remember thinking of sex at all around them. I was working off an adrenalin high while they were in the vicinity. Lucky you, though, I will have to look them up online to see who they are. Not that it matters, from what Thom says, they have the patriarch of Klinger International asking questions and being stonewalled by our good friend Mr. Proper-By-The-Book Ishmeal. I don't move in the same social circles as the Klingers do either."

She was definitely going to do research on the Klinger family though. The reason for someone deliberately trying to kill a young family like that was lame. Eric Klinger was hiding more than just his video games if she was any judge. She knew several things already. One, he had to carry a gun in his vehicle for protection; two, his wife was a new addition to his life and the baby was most likely the reason for the marriage. She also learned that Liam Klinger had the bluest eyes she'd ever remembered seeing.

Laura smiled and patted her shoulder, "I can see you are tired, honey, I'll sneak back in here with an IPad and we can drool over their pictures together, how's that?" Mackie was asleep, and she leaned over to give the girl a kiss on the head before leaving the room. Her mind continued to dwell on the younger woman as she walked through the hospital corridors with her security detail close by.

Later, at home with Thom, while they ate take-out burgers and fries, she told him what she was thinking. "I want to give Mackie a chance to find a man of her own. I know I was lucky to find you, and men with your tolerance and understanding are few and far between, but she deserves better than life has given her so far."

Thom Hurrell knew what she was up to, just not who the sacrificial goat was that she had in mind to feed their young friend. "Look, I want her to find happiness too. You should have seen the way Klinger and his men looked at her, even while she was laid out on the furniture. Men find her sexy, but they also become intimidated as soon as she shows her competence and strength. Remember how you used to drive normally sane men to drink? Now think of you with big guns and toys that blow stuff up. Two things guaranteed to give a man a stiffy. But, sweetheart, the men want to be the ones using the toys while the little lady stands behind him and cheers him on." He got a French fry thrown at him for being such a downer.

"I think that I'll need a female bodyguard for the next few months, you know how busy it gets just before Halloween. So many parties and events I should attend, but you always hated. Mackie can accompany me, and you can wait for me at home with your devilish smile and naked body. Or, you can come with us and steer good looking hard bodied men Mackie's way."

He grinned, "You still think you can stand to see this old body naked?"

She knew he was teasing her as he stood and clasped her upper arm in his big hand, but that was part of the ritual. As soon as they got near the bed, she began inspecting her old man. She took her time undressing the big man, and his grin inspired her as she went to her knees to place soft kisses on his prick and thighs. "I can't find a flaw, there is no way you can be as old as you are. Isn't it nice, junior looks happy to see me." She palmed his balls and gently gave them a squeeze. "Hello, boys, feeling good here."

He shivered as her mouth closed around his prick, and he knew he would never get used to that first little nibble that made him groan every time. He loved the feelings she brought out in him, always had loved them. He loved her, period. And there was nothing he wouldn't do for his girl, and he knew she felt the same for him. He grunted as she brought him relief, and when he caught his breath, he pulled her to the bed and proceeded to show her who her master was. He knew she loved having his mouth on her pink flesh, he licked and sucked at her sweet pussy until his prick became long and hard again, before he crawled his way up over her beautiful lush body and seated himself deep inside her clenching flesh.

She was so beautiful, and she was his.

Mackie was released from the hospital three days after she was admitted. She no longer had a home to go to, and wondered which motel in the area had weekly rates. Ishmeal waited at the curb for her to be discharged and he seemed in a good mood as he shut the door behind her and slid into the driver's seat of the Crown Vic.

"You know, Maxine, you really should think about retiring, and this time actually do it. It's not personal, but it does get monotonous picking you up from the hospital in various places. Wasn't the last time in St. Mary's, and the time before that was in Mexico City if I remember correctly." He glanced at her before resuming driving through the traffic of downtown Kalamazoo. "I am only saying this because sooner or later, I won't be the one picking you up. It will be the funeral home director. Because, well, no matter how tough you look and act, there is always someone who is tougher and meaner than you out there. I've become rather fond of you and would hate to help bury you." He kept staring out of the front window while he talked and Mackie felt touched by his speech.

They got on 131 and headed east. "Thank you for your concern, I didn't deliberately set out either of those times or this one, to rescue anybody. I was sitting in the house minding my own business when the car crash happened. You would be shocked to know I was reading an erotic romance at the time, and just as they were getting into the good squishy, mushy stuff, the crash interrupted the fantasy, the noise was pretty loud. It kinda pisses me off, now I'll never get to finish that book."

Ishmeal laughed, and Mackie was startled to hear the sounds coming from him. She had heard his quick chuckles over the years, but never a full blown laugh like this. She couldn't help but smile at him, Ishy was usually easy to rouse into his pissy mode, but now she knew his secret, he could laugh. "So where are you taking me today? Because the last thing I remember is that I no longer have a home, clothes, or even a mailbox."

Chapter 6

It didn't surprise her when they pulled into the circular driveway at the Senator's home. Thom and Laura had become the best friends a woman like her could possibly have. Ishy had an indulgent look on his face when Laura ran down the steps to greet her, and the look made Mackie realize the man had it bad for the Senator. *Talk about defeated before beginning, geez*, as far as she knew Ishy had been with the General since birth, or whatever the pecking order of the Army's assignments were. It stood to reason he would become fond of the people he was around everyday for years, but the look he was sending toward Laura, if Thom ever saw it, the younger man would be in trouble, big trouble.

Laura's voice made her turn and pay attention to what she said. "I am so glad you're going to be my protection detail from now on, at least until the end of the holidays, with you around I can have some fun."

Mackie returned the tight embrace and had to smile. It would have been nice if someone had asked her if she had any other plans for the next few months, but truthfully, she was happy. She always stayed at the Senator's place when she was assigned to provide protection for her, but since she had retired from the job, "I'm not objecting here, but you do realize that you'll be footing the bill for me as a private bodyguard right? Even with the family discount I'm not cheap."

That statement got her a scowl from Ishmeal, but Laura laughed. "That's not a problem, Mackie, as far as that goes, you are a tax deduction, ta da, problem solved. Believe me, you will be earning your pay, no one is trying to kill me as of right now that I know about, but you get to play dress up with me and go to the forty plus parties I am scheduled to attend between now and New Years."

It was Ishy's turn to grin when she scowled at her assignment. She wanted to stomp her foot and say 'Hell NO', but she wasn't going to and they all knew it.

John was ready for the reception. His suit was hung up and he'd just finished taking a long hot shower. He reached for his boxer briefs, when Darryl walked into the room with his shirt in his hand and somewhere along the way he must have shed his shoes, because he was barefoot. He hadn't seen John yet, and was working on unbuckling his belt and dealing with the zipper on his jeans, when he looked up to see John staring at him.

"Hey, I know Liam's going to kill me for making us late, but I needed to check on some information on our mystery lady."

He dropped his pants and John could see that Darryl wasn't wearing underwear, as usual. The mention of Mackie got his attention away from Darryl's tattooed muscles, and he asked, "What have you found out about her? Liam said the General refuses to talk to him, and even his family name isn't getting the information he wants."

Darryl didn't want to tell his friend that he had very little to tell him, and walked over to the bed where John was sitting.

He sat down next to him and put his arm around John. "We'll find her, there can't be that many women like her with the same name and abilities. If all else fails I'll put a couple of men on to do surveillance of the Senator's place. Senator Downs is married to our friend the General, and from what little I found out an hour ago, that's where the gunshot wounds came from. She was the Senator's bodyguard when she was shot. It stands to reason the General would put Liam in his place when he was busy worrying about a woman that saved his wife's life.

He pulled John's face around to his to kiss his lips. "Liam can wait for a few, what do you think?" He didn't wait for an answer, his lips were again on John's and the men eased back on the bed in a tight embrace. Their hard cocks rubbed together and hips moved in an effort to bring pleasure to each other while enjoying the movement of their bodies. Darryl pushed himself up on his hands and trailed his tongue and lips down the middle of John's chest. "You smell great, man, hmmm." His fingers held John's hard cock and when his lips took over the strong massage on the soft flesh covering hard muscle, John gave a strangled groan.

His hands were busy running down Darryl's back and grasping a handful of the big man's thick hair. "Oh fuck yes. Do you have any idea how great that feels?" He ran his hand down to Darryl's cock and began sliding the shaft between his fingers.

They were twenty minutes late, but the look Liam sent them made both men smile and laugh out loud once it dawned on him why they had been delayed. He had rolled his eyes and given them the look, and that kept the grins on their faces until he smiled too.

"You could have waited for me you know, I've been so busy with work and looking for our lady that I haven't had time to do more than drain the pipes in the shower, and let me tell you, it sucks."

The five inch heels on her feet did fantastic things for her ego. She stood in front of the full length mirrored doors in her bedroom and checked out her appearance in detail. The small semi-auto causing a slight bulge on her left front side was barely noticeable. The simple black dress showed a small amount of cleavage, and in her opinion, too much leg, but Laura insisted the dress was perfect for her. Her hair had been professionally styled and hung smoothly over her shoulders. She wasn't crazy about the way the wrist length sleeves of the dress clung to her arms, but she had to admit the person who designed the garment was some kind of genius. This dress made her look almost sexy, which gave her a laugh. She was the least sexually active person she knew.

Laura looked gorgeous and the General was hovering over his territory with a scowl at any man who he perceived to be a possible threat to his property. Especially after last week when an overzealous activist had crashed the cocktail party they had attended. Mackie had dealt with the man, and since it wasn't the first time someone had approached the woman they thought was the Senator, she had been able to take care of the situation before many people noticed the man's rants about the war in the Middle East. She had steered the guy out into the foyer of the building by pretending to want privacy for the discussion. When the Security Personnel finally realized that there was a problem, they hauled him away from the vicinity.

This was a bigger party than last week's had been, and Mackie stayed close to her charge, but not so close that people would remark on the resemblance between the women. She was a decoy, it wasn't the first time she'd assumed the role, and from the looks of Laura's appointment calendar, this was just the beginning of the party season. Next week was Halloween, and knowing that one of the parties would be a masquerade would make it even more difficult for security.

She smiled, remembering how Laura had forced the big bad Army General to sit with them and watch a Bette Midler film about Halloween and witches last night. He'd flatly refused to allow his wife to dress as one of the witches for the masquerade party. Mackie had grinned when he tossed his wife over his shoulder as if they were in their twenty's instead of their late forty's, and smacked her on the ass. "You're enough of a witch without the ugly make-up when you are in a mood. I refuse to allow you to force me to look at the woman I love with a big green wart on her chin, and ratty clothes. Now say goodnight to the nice lady, we are going to bed."

Mackie was still grinning at them when Laura raised her head from the middle of his back and waved her way. "Goodnight."

Several people approached the handsome couple, and everything seemed to be going smoothly so far. There were several diplomats and plenty of security here tonight, so she should have been able to relax, but for some reason, she couldn't. She happened to glance up, and saw a man crouched behind a thick newel post at the top of the open staircase. It could be a person from the security detail, but they were normally not as furtive as this figure was acting. Mackie quickly made her way to the General's side and signaled him with a slight nod of her head. Other than a narrowing of his eyes, he made no sign the interruption of their evening was more than a scheduling problem.

"Well I'm afraid it's time for us to scoot, darling, we're already late for our next stop and if we arrive much later, they might not allow us in the door." He hustled her from the room as quickly as possible, and Mackie watched them drive away before she went back inside the building.

Her number one priority was safe, now she needed to find a dark corner and wait for an opportunity to speak with the influential hosts. The party was being thrown by one of the manufacturers of Drone technology. The stock of the company was rising rapidly with the uses for drones increasing into the private sector, and she cursed herself for not remembering the rest of the details concerning the company. Her only excuse was lack of time to completely study the dossier that she'd been given last night. Her initial perusal of the file had been routine, but Laura had several appointments to be at today, and time management wasn't exactly the Senator's top priority.

She watched the stairs to see if the figure of the man could still be seen lurking, but there was no one there. If there was one time in her life she hoped that her intuition was wrong, she hoped it would be now, but the hairs on her neck and arms were standing at attention, and she needed to move. She asked a passing waiter where the host was tonight. "It's such a crush, and if I don't find him before the party's over, I'll be in big trouble." The older man smiled at the woman towering over him and directed her to a spot twenty feet over to her right. She thanked him and began making her way through the people, listening for anything that might clue her into trouble.

There were two men standing side by side in the center of the small crowd of people. Both men were tall, over six feet, but the older man was at least two inches shorter than the younger man. It was obvious they were father and son. They reminded her of someone, but she didn't have time to search her brain for the recognition that it would require to figure out. The oldest gentleman spied her and assumed she was Senator Downs. She could tell he was happy Laura Downs had made an appearance and was even approaching him to speak. It would have been true enough had Laura stayed at the party. She always made it a point to be gracious and thank her hosts everywhere they went.

"Ah, the lovely Senator Downs has decided to grace our little get together. Allow me to introduce my son, Drummond Klinger." As she shook the hand offered, the name registered and she smiled in a more friendly way. Her fingers were given a harder squeeze and she realized the old boy thought she was flirting with him. Well, she would use that as an excuse to speak with them privately.

"Gentlemen, you have a lovely party, with so many people wishing you well in your endeavors, I haven't had a moment to speak with you in private on a subject the General has told me you have made inquires about. If I could have just a minute?" She smiled and widened her eyes, as they excused themselves from the four men staring at them in speculation. They walked to a semi private corner, and she leaned toward them.

"I am sorry, but I am not the Senator, she and her husband, the General, just left. I wanted to alert you to a possible intruder I saw earlier, just in case he isn't one of your security team. There was a man wearing black clothing crouched on the highest landing of the stairs a few minutes ago, and since he is no longer there, I would urge you to get your security people looking for him. I have counted at least eighteen high profile people here tonight, and most are still in this room."

Mason Klinger narrowed his eyes at her, she was certain his minions in the boardroom shook in fear at the look, but she was not his minion. "Who are you, young lady, and how did you get past our security?"

She grinned at the tone of his voice, but answered his question, "I am Senator Downs' personal security guard, I assess any and all possible threats to her well being." She looked directly at Drummond Klinger, "My name is Maxine Vaught, I think you might have heard the name before."

She bowed her head acknowledging the men and stepped back, before walking toward the front doors. Her self-appointed task was done. If she was mistaken, they might be a bit pissy, but if she was right, and there was a threat, they would know it was there.

The puzzle of why Eric had been a target made perfect sense now. Drones were just interactive videogames, controlled by remote flight simulators, and the younger man developed those games. *Ha, and she didn't even need to research that out. Score one for her*. She needed to speak with the General about something else too.

Liam was trying to make his way through the crowd of people to see who it was they were having such a cozy chat with. When she walked away from the elders, he would've sworn it was the woman who mocked him in his dreams. By the time he made it to the men, she was gone. They were scowling and leaning close to each other. "What happened?"

His father looked almost relieved to see him. "We might have an issue, it seems Senator Downs' bodyguard saw someone creeping around on the second floor, the Senator left immediately and the guard stayed to warn us. She just left. We are trying to decide what the best course of action we should take without causing a riot."

"Well first, I know Darryl Reynolds is upstairs, I just saw him heading that way a few minutes ago, so I think we need to sit tight until he reports in. If he tells us to get people moving out, we'll worry about it then." Thoughts of Maxine Vaught left as he considered the best way to move three hundred people out of the building without causing a panic.

His cell vibrated and he checked to see who the message was from. "Situation neutralized, party on!" Darryl was being witty.

"It looks like there was an intruder, Darryl says party on, so he has the intruder in custody." His father was looking at him strangely, and he asked, "What?"

Now that Drummond had met the woman who had saved his nephew and his family, and had also saved Liam, he could see the attraction she inspired in his son. She was a beautiful woman. Statuesque, curved, and self-assured. The woman was capable with weapons and after tonight, he had to add that she was a very observant trained security guard.

"Oh nothing, son, we briefly met your mystery GI Jane." Mason Klinger was eighty-two years old, but he acted like a man half his age most of the time, especially around beautiful women. "You should grab ahold of that one, sonny, she has, well, let me just say I wouldn't kick her out of my bed if I could talk her into it."

He knew it, the woman he'd spied earlier *was* Mackie. At least he now knew she was in the area. If she were a member of Senator Downs' security team, it would explain a few things. It also gave him a way to contact her. His grandfather was right, if he got her into his bed, he planned to make it a memorable experience for both of them.

The woman was a mystery and he had been trying to find her for too damn long. She had been impossible to forget, and after a few nights of drinking and talking, his friends told him the same woman was haunting their dreams. As Darryl put it.

"She was like what I always imagined an Amazon or Valkyrie would have been back in the day. I tried to make it to her before Tyler shot her, but I was on the other side of Eric's SUV when I heard the shot. I looked up and started running, but it was too late." He'd shaken his head, as baffled as Liam had been at the time. "I keep dreaming about that face of hers, the scars, the whole thing, and let me tell you, if I ever get her near a bed and she'd healthy, I'm not surfacing for a week. I can't dig up much on the woman, but I'd bet she has one hell of a story, if she were to share it."

Liam agreed, right down to the week long bed stint. John had been researching scars and had identified most of Mackie's injuries to his own satisfaction, and had shared his findings with both of them. The three of them had then made a timeline and cross-referenced the information in the reports like any good stalkers would do. Officially she was considered a semi-retired security consultant, yet they could find no contact information, and her trail went cold when she left the hospital.

They'd met her, now that they knew where to find her, they would need to find out more about her, and from the one meeting they'd had, getting ideas on how to integrate her into their sphere wasn't going to be easy. Then again, they didn't want easy, they wanted a permanent partner.

Chapter 7

It hadn't taken him long to call, was her first thought. Mackie had been waiting to see if he would take advantage of knowing where she could be contacted. Now she knew that Liam was as interested in her as she was with him. When he'd called this morning, she was still surprised he asked her to meet with him at Drysdale's Pub & Brew House. He must want this meeting to be a personal one, and she was nervous for the first time in a very long time. It had been so long since she'd been on a real date with a man that she couldn't remember it. The man was as forgettable as the events on that date.

This date was different, she was already attracted to Liam Klinger. The only fly in the ointment so to speak was that she had also been thinking about Darryl Reynolds and of course the gorgeous Dr. John Fielding, almost as much as she'd thought about Liam Klinger.

She had the advantage of knowing who they were to begin with, and had done background checks on all three men. Darryl Reynolds was forty-one years old, and six foot three inches tall. From the pictures she'd seen, she knew he had several intricate tattoos decorating his thickly muscled shoulders, arms, and back. He probably outweighed the other two in just muscle alone. He had blue eyes and close-cropped brown hair and a set of lips that gave her thoughts that were X-rated. He was also a former Navy SEAL. He was divorced and had two half-siblings that still contacted him when they wanted something. His reputation in the industry was impeccable in the security community.

Dr. John Fielding was thirty-eight years old, six foot four, and by her estimation two hundred thirty pounds. Blue eyes and his hair was a light brown, almost blond in color. He was considered a bit of a genius. He had served in a field hospital during the invasion of Iraq, and added a second tour in Afghanistan. He was graceful, and watching him workout on the horse and rings in the video she'd seen had been a pleasure. He had two groupings of tattoos, but the only one she could make out from the video had puzzled her. His forte as she'd read was in researching antidotes and developing vaccines against chemical weapons.

Liam Kennedy Klinger was the second son born to Drummond and Teresa Klinger. His older brother was Thornton Kennedy Klinger. From all accounts even the sister, Carla, was saddled with their mother's maiden name of Kennedy for a middle name.

He was six feet four inches tall, thirty-six years old, and had reddish brown hair and blue eyes. He was also built almost as big as Darryl was. He had a few tats on his chest and shoulders, but he didn't have nearly the intricate artwork that Darryl sported. He too had been in the Middle East fighting. Only he hadn't been on the ground, he flew a bomber jet, and had a string of ribbons and medals to match his exploits. When he'd told her the three of them weren't helpless, he hadn't been lying.

The pictures in the dossier on her desk showed the three men at the gym, in a dojo, and in a wrestling ring. She knew that every man owned several guns, and those were just the ones that were registered to them. They were individuals that carried similar traits and each man wore the same tat on their upper chest. A three flamed fire was an unusual tattoo with vivid coloring, and she wondered at the meaning.

No matter how deep she dug, there was no mention of how they met, or any permanent female companions. Rumors and speculations ran from gay to kinky and straight when she spoke to a few people about any of the men. Maybe she would eek out some information on her date, but she wouldn't hold her breath. The best she could hope for would be a pleasant dinner and conversation. At least for tonight.

She walked into the pub and wasn't surprised to see the place was almost filled to capacity. She stood by the door to try to find Liam, but there were too many people blocking her line of sight, and it creeped her out a little. She hated crowds of people. In her profession, a crowd of people could contain who knew how many potential assassins. Deciding to walk further into the room, she began dodging waitresses and people balancing drinks in an effort to get to their tables without spilling the contents of the glasses. She glanced toward the bar and saw a tall man with a moustache and bald head waving his fingers at her to keep going to the back of the room. She pointed at herself and he nodded his head and smiled. She smiled back and kept walking.

Liam must have asked the man to watch out for her and direct her to his table. It was a nice thing for him to do, and for some reason, the knowledge made her feel warm inside. She still hadn't seen Liam in any of the booths or at the scattered tables as she was almost to the back wall when her arm was grasped just above the elbow of her right side. She stopped in her tracks and slowly looked to see if she should have cause for concern.

"Liam asked me to bring you to the room, this place is always a crush on Friday nights. I told the dumbass that he should have picked a less popular place to have this meeting, but he figured that you would want to be in a public place the first time. And by the way, you look beautiful tonight." Darryl Reynolds was talking and almost mowing people down as he pulled her along through the short hallway and she was surprised she hadn't questioned his presence.

He didn't even stop when they reached one of the small meeting rooms, he just opened the door and almost shoved her inside the room before he came in behind her and shut and locked the door. "Now she's wondering if I'm going to try to kill her or fuck her. I told you that you should have picked a place that would be quieter," Darryl said to Liam, even as he took her arm again and escorted her to the table and pulled out a chair for her to sit in, before scooting her forward and sitting in a chair on the opposite side of the table.

The only thing on the table was a leather soft-side file case, and an electronic notebook. There were no drinks, not even a bowl of popcorn in the room, and she was getting the impression that she had been lured here for something other than for Liam to whisper sweet words into her shell like ears. Fuck, just her luck to be attracted to someone who wanted to use her for reasons other than a bed partner. Men like these didn't go for scarred oversized women with brains, and she should have known better than to allow vanity to override reality.

So much for Laura's giddy excitement that the handsome Mr. Klinger was romantically interested in Mackie. She's chatted along as they finally picked out the pretty royal blue dress that was short enough to be fashionable, yet long enough not to show her ass when she sat down. The five inch heels did awesome things for her legs and the way she walked too.

Liam was still on the phone talking in French, if she wasn't mistaken, and she was about done with this charade. It had been a good ten minutes since she'd walked into the room and sat down. She turned her inquiring eyes toward Darryl. "Is this a business meeting? I must have gotten the wrong impression when Mr. Klinger called earlier. I haven't eaten dinner, being under the assumption that food would be on the schedule. So if you don't mind, we can reschedule this meeting for another time. My stomach thinks my throat's been slit, and it is making me aware that I haven't eaten since early this morning. Call me tomorrow and I will try to fit you in my schedule for a meeting." She stood and walked toward the door. *So much for a romantic evening, this was a big waste of time.*

The old saying "for a big man, he sure moves fast" filtered through her mind, as Darryl Reynolds hand hit the doorknob before she had it in her outstretched hand. She turned her head and waited for his explanation before she did something physical to him that she might regret later.

"Settle down there, Liam is talking to his grandmother. Isabella Kennedy never stops talking until she is ready, and Liam loves the old girl so he let's her compromise his time. You can understand that, can't you?"

She turned around and folded her arms over her chest and stared at Darryl for a moment, then turned her gaze toward Liam. His face was almost comical as he rolled his eyes and listened to the person on the other end of the airwaves. He was nodding his head and she almost burst into laughter as he made a rolling gesture with his empty hand, another eye roll and she had to put her hand over her mouth as she choked on her laughter.

Darryl met her eyes and nodded his head. "She speaks English as well as one born to it, but insists on speaking in French because she has decided it is the only civilized language left in the modern world." He nodded his head toward Liam who was pacing back and forth, now holding the bridge of his nose and shaking his head. "The interesting part is that Liam doesn't speak French other than a few phrases that he learned in high school, and few of those phrases are something you would want to say to a ninety-four-year-old grandmother. Even if she was a former burlesque showgirl back in the late nineteen thirties and early forties."

Mackie couldn't stop the giggles, her eyes were tearing up from the pressure being held back from shouting in laughter. She had to look away from the pacing man, and she held her hand up to stop Darryl from continuing his explanation. He was still watching Liam and grinning.

She couldn't speak, if she did open her mouth words would have to wait until she was finished laughing. His next comments finished her off, there was no stopping her from laughing out loud.

"Every time she's around, John and I have to keep our backs to the wall. She has a habit of pinching our asses. One time she asked me if I was attracted to older women, and I made the mistake of saying I had met some very attractive ladies of a certain age." He turned his head to watch her laugh and continued, "You can laugh, the old gal scares me. Don't even get me started about her ninetieth birthday celebration. All I will say is that I don't care how rude it might be, I won't sit next to her again. You will have to ask John how it felt to have her lay her hand on his thigh during dinner and squeezing it. He dropped his glass of wine, and she insisted on helping him by dabbing at his crotch with her napkin. I had to get up and leave the room when she invited him to her room at the hotel to change out of his wet pants."

Mackie was laughing out loud and the more he talked the harder and longer she laughed. Her eye make-up was probably leaving mascara trails down her cheeks but she couldn't do anything about it. The old woman sounded like a hoot, and she would give a week's paycheck to see the three men having to deal with a ninety-year-old wild child. She could only say "I, you, oh." Not very coherent at all, but that was the extent of her attempt at conversation.

The shushing sound from across the room just added fuel to the fire. She bent down to pick up her purse to find a tissue, and overbalanced in the five inch heels. Luckily Darryl caught her and held her in his arms for long moments. He pulled a clean handkerchief from his back pocket and wiped her cheeks, all the while telling her more about the little old woman with the libido of a teenager.

"You think that's funny, huh? Well you would have had the guys with the white jackets come and take you away when we had to dance with her at the Governor's Annual Ball. She kept playing grab ass, and Liam had to socialize with the dignitaries while we babysat her. One old guy who had been courting the lovely Isabella for a while, challenged me to a fistfight over the honor of dancing with her. I gave in too easily and she didn't forgive me for that. She sicc'd her dear companion the prissy Mz. Darling on me. Trust me, that woman was the bible thumper from hell. Sadly the delightful lady went to meet her maker last year."

He finished wiping her face and ran the corner of the material under her eyes one last time, and said, "There, good as new." He leaned further down and kissed her lightly on the lips, then placed another whisper soft kiss on the end of her nose before assisting her back to her seat, and retrieving her purse from the floor.

Surprise was the reason she didn't deck him for taking advantage. At least that's what she told herself. She hadn't imagined the kiss, it was brief, but it happened. He had given her more human contact in the few minutes than she'd had in years and she didn't know what to do or say about it. If she examined her feelings about it, she would be forced to admit that she liked feeling feminine. She refused to say or admit she felt almost safe in his arms as he wiped the tears of laughter from her cheeks. It was crazy. She needed to get a hold on herself and stop this shit before she turned into some apron wearing doormat. That wasn't her style. Deciding to ignore what happened was her way of dealing for now and she nodded to herself in reassurance.

She tried to formulate a sentence and decided to continue the topic of Liam's grandmother. Before she opened her mouth, Liam said something that sounded like well spoken French to her untrained ears, "*Grand-mère, s'il te plait, arrêtes d'appeler l'infirmière par des noms coquins, et tu ne devrais pas pincer les fesses de John le jardinier. Sois sage, et je viendrais te voir le mois prochain. Je t'aime,*" and pushed the button to end the call. He tossed the phone on the table and she had to smile at the way his hands went to his hair and he pulled two fist fulls away from his head and groaned.

His hair spiked upwards and Darryl laughed. She turned her head to hide a smile. This had to be one of the strangest evenings she'd participated in for as long as she could remember. Who knew that these men were such comedians? Darryl had purposefully made her laugh, but Liam was unaware of the picture he presented to his audience. The hair spikes resembled short red toned horns and his face was red from whatever his grandmother had said at the end of their conversation.

Darryl spoke up and brought Liam's attention back to the people in the room. "You're horns are showing man, the sweet Isabella giving you advice again?"

Liam flipped him the bird and Darryl laughed out loud for the first time, and Mackie had to smile at his enjoyment at Liam's expense.

Liam shook his head and gave her a long look, before holding out his hand expecting her to take it in hers. When she gave hers into his hand, he pulled her to her feet and stared at her for a heartbeat before pulling her closer and bending to kiss her lightly on the lips.

What was it with these men that they thought it was all right to randomly kiss her any way? "Okay, was there a reason for that? Or are you planning to give me bad news and want to soften the effect?"

The way he smiled with a short laugh gave her inappropriate thoughts, and she tamped down the attraction she was feeling. Obviously he had invited her here for something other than a dinner date, and she would be smart to pay attention instead of mooning over the two handsome men.

Darryl cleared his throat and reached into the leather file case. He fingered through the files until he picked the one he was looking for and drew it out of the rest. He opened the chosen file and looked at Liam for confirmation. He got the nod and passed the file folder to Mackie.

"Before we go any further here, we need you to read this and sign it if you feel agreeable to the terms. It's a non-disclosure contract, and covers any and all information and includes both personal and business confidentiality clauses. If you have any questions, or wish to have your legal representative, then by all means we can reschedule tonight's date."

Oh for Christ's sake, all five pages of the verbiage did exactly that. She wasn't to discuss Liam Klinger, his representatives, co-workers, friends of the family and especially family members. Good Lord, it was like the non-disclosures she had signed over and over during her years of security. Only this one extended to family and friends. Once she read it through, she wrote on the bottom of the contract the same sentence she'd written over and again over the years.

"Agreed with the caveat: Illegal activities in any form will be exempt from contractual obligation."

She initialed the handwritten sentence, and signed on the designated line. "Here you go." She pushed the file back to Darryl, who in turn slid it to Liam who looked at the last page at what she'd written into the contract and nodded his head with a small smile.

She was ready to get this dog and pony show on the road, she was hungry, and even if curiosity was eating her alive from the inside out, if they didn't get to the point of this "date" she would be forced to leave and find food.

Liam answered one of her questions without her having to open her mouth. "We're just waiting for John to get here, and then we can move this evening forward." He picked up his cell phone and checked it for messages. "He knew what time to be here, for Christ's sake, I know he's been busy, but damn, he could make the effort."

The rapping on the door had Darryl moving toward it, with his hand reaching behind his back, and Mackie wondered how she'd missed seeing that he was carrying in the small of his back. She wondered what was going on, but decided to go ahead and play with the big boys for a few. It would take her mind off her stomach at least. She stood and unclipped the beautiful decorative buckle from her belt and calmly walked over to the opposite side of the door that Darryl had silently unlocked. He reached for the doorknob and she shook her head at his gesture.

She laid the end of the small square on the metal handle, and Darryl pulled his hand back, grinned, and asked, "Who is it?" The answer was muffled and the visitor pounded on the door again. When the handle began to turn, Mackie raised her eyebrow at Darryl. His shrug and free hand gestured for her to go ahead, she pressed the button on the side of the box. An arc of electricity showed on the metal, but the cursing and thud on the other side of the door was what interested her.

Liam's phone vibrated on the table, and he picked it up to read the message. He frowned as he read the message. "Fuck, John says he has two flat tires and someone tried to hack his computer. He's meeting us in ten." He shoved the file into the case and placed the notebook inside, between the other folders, snapped the clasp, and told the two by the door, "Let's go."

Darryl took her arm and guided her to Liam, while he went to the table and pushed in the chairs and looked at the room with a critical eye to make certain there was nothing to see if the person on the other side of the door was a legitimate lost patron and called for assistance.

Liam pulled her behind him as he pushed the wall near the corner of the room and it swung into a narrow hallway. He sent her inside first and he and Darryl followed quickly behind her and pushed the panel back in place. Liam flipped two dead bolt locks on the top and bottom of the door, and used a scissor lock to secure the middle of the door. Noises could almost immediately be heard from the other side of the wall and from the sounds coming from the room, someone was not at all happy to have missed his prey.

Mackie was impressed, but it wasn't the time to praise or question the two men. She followed Liam, while Darryl followed her down the passageway single file. The only light was the LED penlight Liam had produced from his pocket, but it showed enough light for them to navigate the small space.

They came to another turn in the path, when Liam stopped and listened for a moment, before reaching up and turning what appeared to be a small faucet. The wall slid aside and he looked into the darkened room before stepping inside. He found a lamp and illuminated the room in a soft dim light, before his companions stepped through the doorway.

Darryl shut the wall panel behind them and kicked the silver colored wall decoration nearby where the panel closed.

They heard a toilet flush and water running, before the door opened to reveal John standing there. He nodded to the men, but he smiled toward Mackie. "Good evening, beautiful, nice to see you on your feet without worrying if you're going to collapse at any minute." He came close to her and leaned in to steal a quick kiss, before turning to the others and starting to talk about his delay.

Chapter 8

Before he could get started on his no doubt in depth explanation, she had to say something. "All right, I get that you have a security breech or worse. The one problem I am having right this minute is that I need to eat something, this is not an option, and the first one of you that tells me to live off the land is going down the hard way so I will have something soft to land on. I get fed or I walk out of here on my own to find something to eat."

John looked at her and seemed to know that she meant business. "Didn't you tell them that you have Hypoglycemia?"

She shook her head. "You tell me, what business is it of theirs to begin with? I told them I was hungry and had skipped lunch thinking I was meeting Liam for dinner. It never occurred to me that I would be going through a rat maze and being forced to fight off the nausea while you all decide whether I need to eat or not." John looked toward his friends with a scowl, but she had had enough.

"You know what? Fuck this, I can find my own food." She went to the door and opened it, stepped into a beautiful wooden paneled room, and saw the strangest little man pushing a cart of food into the room from the opposite doorway. She knew it was food from the smell alone, and wasted no time striding over to the cart, stopping his forward motion so she could lift the lid from one of the plates. The plate she'd chosen had a selection of appetizers on it and she felt her fingers singe as she picked up a crostini topped with cheese and some kind of spicy smelling sausage. She blew on the hot treat until she hoped it was cool enough to chew and took a small bite. Within seconds that had gone down and she made short work of the rest of the crunchy bred, before taking a small semi-circle Quesada and devouring that too. She next reached for another of the spicy circles and got her hand smacked for her efforts. The little man had smacked her with a spoon, and she was not in the mood to be fucked around with.

"Do that again, and I will put your little ass through a wall. Now back off, before I get mean." She reached for the snack again and he hit her again.

"Lady, you can wait for the other's to arrive, show some manners while you're a guest in this house. Or better yet leave. I don't know how you got in here, but the door is that way, I'll be happy to escort you there." He stood back and pulled the hem of his vest down as if he planned to show her who was the boss. And it damned sure wasn't her.

She put both hands on the edge of the cart and glared at him. "I will leave when the host asks me too, or I feel like leaving, so unless you own the place, I suggest you back off, I don't care if you are the size of a ten-year-old or not. I need to eat, and you need to leave me the hell alone while I do it."

The little man glared right back at her, and any other time she would have admired his tough guy act, now was not a good time. She picked up the round bread again and he calmly walked over to her and kicked her in the knee from behind. She fell forward onto the cart and barely caught herself from falling onto the food and crashing the entire meal.

"I might be the size of a ten-year-old, but my ass isn't the first thing people see when they look my way you freeloader. Tell me, Amazon, has there ever been a man who looks into your eyes when he introduces himself? They probably stare at those gallon jugs you carry around on your chest. Maybe I should let you go ahead and fill your face until you have fattened up even more."

The evil little shit knew how to verbally bring a woman her size to her knees, that was for sure, and if she wasn't about to pass out, she would trade verbal insults with him all night. She turned back to the cart and lifted another lid. Too late, he came at her and she turned too suddenly to stop herself from falling to her knees and slowly falling the rest of the way just as she'd feared. She heard men laughing as she went down and cursed the entire gender, "Fuckers." Her head was spinning too badly for her to do anything to help herself. The shaking that she had been feeling internally now consumed her body and she felt strong arms picking her up from the hard wooden floor to place her on a lounger.

"Dammit, what the hell is wrong with her?" Liam was yelling at John, as Darryl moved her from the floor to the settee.

John was busy rummaging on the cart to see what could be used to bring her blood sugar back up to where she could cope until they got something healthy into her. "She told you that she needed to eat, she has what's commonly referred to as low blood sugar, and it is rare for adults to have it. Some people metabolize sugars at a high rate of speed and without snacking between meals most of them will feel faint or nauseous. She should be carrying a high carb snack in case of emergencies, but most women in dressy clothes wouldn't think to toss a snack in her handbag. Ha, here we go, sugar will do it. I don't keep glucose tablets in my bag. Dorian, you evil little fucker, why were you trying to stop her from eating?"

He mixed the sugar cubes with water forming a small amount of thick liquid sugar water then crossed the room to where Mackie was stretched out. He sat next to her and tried to spoon the concoction into her mouth without success. He ended up pulling her bottom lip out and dropping a small amount of the sugar into each side of her teeth. Her saliva and the heat from her mouth should help the energy travel to where it needed to be. The tremors stopped after a few minutes, but she remained out of it.

Dorian, John's houseman, was staring at the troublemaker. "How was I to know that the cow was allowed to graze through the dinner I was setting out for you and the guys? She fell on the food like it was the first meal she'd seen in weeks, and looking at her, that is plainly not the case."

Liam advanced on the man and Dorian watched him coming toward where he stood, and beat a hasty retreat into the direction of the kitchen. Liam had him by the shoulders before he made it four feet.

Liam usually got a kick out of the smart mouthed little man. He admired him and his work ethic, but this behavior and attitude toward Mackie was going to be stopped before any more time passed. He crouched down to his knees to talk to him.

"Dorian, the three of us need that woman, and we happen to have personal interests in her too. If you can't be civil to her, then we will need to make other arrangements. Or we can retire you a few years earlier than planned. She'll be around for a very long time if we have anything to say about it, and it could get awkward if I ever hear you call her names like that again. It pisses me off and from the look on Darryl's face when you called her a cow, you should be happy it was me who grabbed you. She saved our lives a few months back, and she risked her life to save Eric and his new family too."

Liam let go of the shorter man's shoulders and stood to his full height. "You've been a loyal and good friend to have around for the past few years, but the attitude changes now, or pack your things and I'll cut you a check."

Dorian was stunned, not only by the threat of forced retirement. This was the person who saved Eric? The other men were big boys and could take care of themselves, so he had no doubt Liam was exaggerating about her saving their lives. Eric had told him that someone named Mack had pulled his wife and that precious baby, EJ, from the wreckage and then came back for him. This is the Mack he spoke of, the one who had taken a shot trying to keep him safe?

He had helped raise Eric, and the young man was as loved by him as any child he might have gotten from his own wife, had she been able to have children. Now he was going to help Eric and Jenny raise the little one, and planned to tell the doctor tonight that he was leaving his employ and why.

He saw that the woman was sitting up and holding her head in her palms, and tried to formulate the words to thank her for saving his boy, but words meant very little compared to what he was feeling. Liam and Darryl were watching him, and he nodded toward the men before walking over to where John was keeping an eye on her.

"The next time you're in need of anything, just ask. I apologize for the name calling, but you are part of the blame for this too you know. Since these oversized bears forgot to tell me that you would be joining them for dinner, they can accept part of the blame too. I have things to do, so I will say goodnight."

He turned to John and told him, "We have things that need to be talked about, I'll see you tomorrow." He straightened his vest and left the room.

Darryl grinned, "One of these days that little asshole is going to open his mouth and someone is going to glue it shut. He's always got to have the last word, and damned if he wasn't right in a way. He's probably gonna lecture you on manners again, it was fun the last time from what you told us."

John shook his head and informed them, "Nah, he has been plotting to leave me and can't wait to pack his suitcase. He's planning to be Eric Junior's nanny, with a lot of encouragement from the baby's father and grandfather." He shot Liam a dirty look, after all it was his nephew who was stealing the best caretaker he'd ever employed. "You know how it is, who can resist shitty diapers and being vomited on at three in the morning. I can't compete with that, so I get left like an old dog at the shelter. The new puppy is more fun."

Darryl didn't bother to try to mask his hilarity this time. He laughed out loud and shook his head. "Jealous over a baby? What the hell is this? You were doing fine before Dorian came along, you can always find another housekeeper, you know. Pouting isn't an attractive look on you, man. You know as well as everyone else does, that man might be little, but he's as lethal as any pit bull. Given recent events, if it was my kid, I'd be doing the same thing."

Dorian rushed back into the room with a tall glass of freshly squeezed orange juice for Mackie, and he took it straight to her. "Here, drink up, and then eat something." He watched as she held the glass to her lips and took a long swallow.

She gave him a small smile and said, "Thank you," he nodded his head and left the room again without looking at the others.

The sugar and juice perked her up enough to pay attention while the men began dishing up their meal, and she thanked Liam for the plate that he handed her.

"So when are you guys planning on telling me why I'm here? And before you give me anything but the truth, I am out of here if I think you're full of crap. I can say this much, it's the strangest dinner date that I've ever agreed to." She took a big bite of the almost cold noodle concoction and waited for someone to begin talking.

Liam finished chewing and swallowing the food in his mouth before saying, "Let's finish eating first, afterwards we can talk. It's complicated and you will play a major role if you agree to our plan."

The room was silent until they began stacking plates on the cart, and Mackie stood to follow John and Darryl into another room. Liam held her back with his hand on her upper arm. "Look, I'm sorry that tonight has been a flat out mess. This is the way life has been for the past few months, and until the reception, we had been looking for you on a strictly personal basis. Afterward, well you'll hear in a few minutes. So, before anything is said you need to know this." He leaned down and embraced her and leaned down to touch her lips with his. His tongue coaxed her to open her lips and she enjoyed the feeling of his full out assault on her mouth. By the time he let her mouth go, his hands were full of the cheeks of her ass and she felt his hard cock pressing into her stomach. As kisses went, she'd give that one a ten.

He left his hand on her arm as they walked into the next room to join Darryl and John. *This must be the war room*, she thought as she sat in the chair Liam had pulled from the table. At least the men had manners, they were all nuts, but nuts with manners went a long way in her book. Looking around the room, she could see this was a favorite sanctuary from the worn furnishings and man toys decorating the shelves. Remote control trucks and sports balls shared a shelf, just as a volume of *The Art of*

War, and a stack of Super Hero comic books did.

She wondered if the men knew that she was only sitting here ready to hear what they had to say because her sense of the ridiculous was beginning to appreciate the evening's strangeness, and she was curious to get the rest of the events underway. She was tired, but nothing was going to stop her from hearing them out after Liam's little teaser. They were all looking at each other, and no one said a word, so she got the ball rolling. "Okay, you have my attention. Let me start by saying you all know how to show a girl a good time, but since it's already ten thirty, why don't you just tell me what's going on and we can go from there?"

Liam gave her a small smile and Darryl nodded his head, John sat with his hands folded on the table and seemed to be watching for her reaction before she'd been told anything.

"This is hard to explain, so bear with me for a minute please." Liam opened a folder from the stack in the center of the table and started talking.

"Klinger International has their fingers in a lot of venues. We have in our portfolio companies that buy and sell everything, from ice cream to pharmaceuticals. As you know, we also do extensive research and development. What you might not know is that Eric was not being stalked and the attempt on his life had nothing to do with the latest video game, we have developed new drone technology and weapons systems for the unmanned machines. The U S Government is very interested in this and we had kept it under wraps until the negotiations and sale can become final.

"The night of the reception when you saw the intruder, Darryl had one of his suspicions and went to follow up on them. The man is one of a group who wants to stop the use of Drone technology combining several other weapons that are being developed such as lasers and smarter smart bombs. His group has ties to terrorist organizations over seas too.

"The man's biggest mistake was in using out of date intel, and not doing his homework. That mansion is a rental, no one lives there. The rooms are there for the event's use and while it is rented on a monthly basis to some people, our contract was for the weekend only. He thought he could snatch one of our family members to keep us from selling the technology. Darryl found him in the closet of what was once the master suite."

Darryl took over the explanation when Liam began pouring beverages for all of them at the small table in the corner of the room that was half filled with bottles. He handed her a glass identical to the rest that he passed to the men. Whiskey neat wasn't her favorite alcoholic drink, but if she was going to play with the big boys, she might as well not bitch too much about the wish for some cola and ice to go with it.

"Last night someone broke into this house, and thanks to Dorian, nothing was tampered with. He woke up when he heard the back door open and thought it was John coming in. Being the evil little shit that he is, Dorian shot the fucker in the kneecap.

"So now we have two would be spies, and more are on their way. According to the first guy, the reward for one of the Klinger's is high, the reward for some of their close employees and associates is just a small amount lower. The one who broke in here wanted John's research in defensive medicine stopped."

Mackie grinned and shook her head. "Do you mean to tell me that you have at least two factions working against Klinger Corporation? It sounds to me like you have more than one security breach, and given the scope of your company's reach, ferreting out the moles could be close to impossible." She was quiet for a few moments, before continuing, "So the threats are all geared to stopping the technology, but what if it is just a ruse to keep you so busy guarding your people, that you stop all research and development for a time? Long enough for some enterprising thief to find out where you keep the actual technology and steal it. Which leads me to think your problem is a close advisor and someone you consider a loyal friend.

"I assume tonight's adventure was a test?"

All three men nodded their heads and Liam rubbed the back of his neck, shot John a look, and turned his head to give Darryl the same look. They all sat down in a cluster with her at the table. Something gave her a warning that she wasn't going to like what they had in mind for her participation in catching the person responsible.

Darryl again started talking as Liam pushed several photographs toward her. John remained silent, but watched her intently. His perusal made her uncomfortable, but she was certain her discomfort didn't show. What in the hell were they up to?

Chapter 9

"Today we held a conference with four of the top executives at Klinger. I mentioned that I would be there at the Pub tonight and hoped that a certain lady would show up. I never mentioned a name or said anything else about it. In the mean time, Liam was in the corner of the room making plans to meet you tonight. He never told me who he was meeting until we met in the hallway at the condo. I wasn't aware that he had a date and it was too late to call you and cancel. I was trying to trap our snitch, I didn't plan to meet anyone. Once we'd established that we were dumbasses, Liam took the passageway into the private room, and as you know, I met you in the bar.

"Taking me out of the picture would be a big blow to Klinger, and now we have four prime suspects. Unfortunately, you are now added in the mix." He reached for her hand and squeezed it gently. "I know it's fucked up reasoning, but the first thing I thought was that I was thankful it was you. You are probably the most capable woman I've met to date, and if anyone can protect herself and others, it has to be you. So I'm sorry you got dragged into our drama, but I swear I'll protect you with my life, and from the little I do know about you, I'm comfortable with knowing you would kill to protect your allies, and the people that you care about."

John spoke up, still staring at her as if gauging her reactions were important to him. "You need to know a few other things. The three of us have an unusual relationship. We have also found that the three of us find you attractive. No matter how I put this it is going to sound strange to you, and I don't blame you if you have a hard time believing me."

Mackie knew that her mouth was hanging open, but what did they expect, to toss that snippet of information in the works?

"No one is saying that we fell head-over-heels-in love at first glance, that's absurd. The truth of the matter is that you interest us, and yes, I am speaking for all three of us. There you stood with a gun pointed at Liam and you would have shot him if our guy hadn't taken you out first. I was semi hard in seconds seeing that 1911 in your hand. I was ready to kill Tyler for shooting you. Liam carried you into the house and helped me undress you. Do you want to know what happened? The sick fucker had a full on hard-on by the time we were done. And I'm not leaving Darryl here out of it. I thought he was going to crawl across the floor and beg the Mistress of Toys that go Boom for permission to kiss your ass. We are all a little crazy, and we're all different than your run of the mill men. Let's face it, you are strong, you have guts, and you are an idealist like each of us are, do you have any idea of how attractive that is for men like us? Any man with blood flowing in his veins would be attracted to you."

He finally smiled and winked at her. She had to look away from that panty wetting grin. That only sent her eyes to see Darryl and Liam both smiling at her as she looked at them in turn.

"The three of us have an intimate relationship, it is a closed group and no other men are allowed, ever. We have intimate relationships with women separately, and we have upon occasion enjoyed passing a night with a woman who liked the idea of having three men to fulfill her fantasies for an evening. There has never been a permanent woman in our lives due to the fact that we have never actually agreed on one woman between the three of us."

John shrugged and looked away for a second and came back to her with the words that told her this was not a ruse. This was real, and she had no idea how to respond.

"We want you, scars and bravery, gadgets, and bossiness. Even that damned cat will be welcomed if you insist on bringing him along. We will do our best to lure you into our lives and hearts. You will be treasured for the rest of our lives, and if you decide you might like a few little clones running around, well, we will know that their mother will protect them with every breath."

Good Lord, this was one of her own fantasies come to life, but what on earth were they thinking? Liam Klinger wasn't exactly low profile, and Darryl Reynolds was well known too. They were almost public figures. John Fielding wasn't as recognizable, but how in the hell would they pull off sharing one woman between the three of them?

"So, just so I have this right. The three of you were discussing me, and my worthiness as a fourth in this strange ménage of lovers?" Nods came her way from the three men. "You have decided that I am an ideal candidate because I have a stupid trait of trying to protect those who I consider vulnerable at the time, like Eric and his family. Yes, I can see the reasoning, but I am not buying the attraction. I have so many scars that I don't even own a swimsuit. The last doctor I saw referred me to a plastic surgeon to take care of the unsightly appearance of my scars." These guys were definitely a few bricks short of a wall. She figured it was time to leave this house of crazies before she started drinking the tainted water. She stood and Darryl stood at the same time. Shit, she was good, she could kick ass when she had to, but he wasn't your average bad guy.

"I think I need to think about this before I give you an answer. I have a job in case you didn't remember. Senator Downs depends on me to keep her safe, and the General would have a few words to say if you tried to shanghai me into leaving her. Why don't I just catch a cab back to the Senator's residence, and I will give you a call in a few days?"

The heads shaking told her that her bid to escape them wasn't going to be as easy as she'd hoped. She was again surprised when Darryl pulled the button up dress shirt apart scattering buttons, and his tie was yanked down and pulled off over his head. The material gave way easily under his thick hands. What arrested her attention was the scars decorating his chest and stomach. He began unbuckling his belt and opened his pants allowing them to drop to his ankles. His legs were bulging with muscles, but the wide scars running over his skin made her want to soothe his pain. He turned around and she saw that the beautiful tattoos she'd admired in the photographs were actually incorporated with the flow of the scars. The dark purples and pinks of the injuries were not masked, they had been used as enhancements to the scenes.

Nothing on earth could have stopped her from reaching out to touch his skin. She traced the scars and followed the patterns until she got to the small of his back. She knew those scars, she knew what had caused them. She had two smaller marks like those above her hips. Someone had burned him with a metal object and allowed it to stay on his flesh, branding him for all time. She didn't think about it, she bent down and placed a kiss on each two inch long brand. He shivered, and she straightened. Her hand found its way to his shoulder and pulled him around to face her again.

"I am so sorry that you had to go through that. You carry the marks of a warrior, and I cannot believe how beautiful you are, scars and all." Her hands pulled him close, hugging him as if she could take away the hellish pain she knew he had endured.

Liam spoke up behind them. "You see the beauty even as horrific as his injuries were. Why would we see anything less than beauty and courage when we saw yours? John carries burn scars on his legs, and the only reason I don't have them is that I flew a plane during my stint in the Air Force. Should we love them less for the scars that they wear?"

Darryl held her close for a few minutes, and let his arms loosen. She stepped back and sat in the chair she'd left. He pulled his pants up, and had to tuck his semi hard cock in before zipping and fastening the closures. He hadn't expected her reaction, and knowing that she didn't find his body ugly, warmed him deep inside.

"At least you didn't run screaming when you saw me almost naked. Does seeing me and my imperfections answer your question about your scars?"

Mackie nodded her head. She was in trouble and she knew it. If the men were bi-sexual, then she could even see where one woman would be a good fit. Her past in security, and... Damn, they had her pegged, and she was starting to believe what they were saying.

"Okay, so I join your family here, what exactly are you getting at? I'll be a target for this traitor and lucky me I can kill a man in two moves with four fingers? Before you say anything, I am not agreeing, I am asking for more specifics so I can make an informed decision to at least part of your plan."

Liam answered her. "I was excited to see you at the reception, and knew that I had to call you. The meeting room wasn't in my plans, but now we have proof that one of the four men is the leak, or mastermind, we still aren't certain. It's my fault that you've been seen with Darryl. But none of it was planned until the last minute. We'll have security feed from the pub to get identities for the people that came after Darryl tonight.

"I had planned to ease you into the idea of being with the three of us. None of us wanted to blurt the entire thing out like this, for Christ's sake. The attraction thing can tie in with the discovery of the spy. The biggest hurdles we faced with you are now explained and out in the open. As for the idea of you going back to work with the Senator, that's not going to be possible."

She gave him a puzzled look and he sighed. "Mackie, think about it. We are after a major Government contract. You working for the Senator, and being seen with one of Klinger's employees could cause the Senator to lose credibility. You have worked for her and protected the woman for years. If you go back to work for her, questions will be asked. As it is, we can either pull it off as a case of you coming to work for us, or you can publicly be a love interest and allow people to speculate as to which one of us you are interested in."

John interrupted and offered his opinion. "We need to talk to the Senator and the General before we move on any of this. He is already aware that we have a breach, but no one outside this room knows how damaging the breach could potentially be. My research hasn't been spoken of outside of the three of us, and the four people in that meeting."

Mackie had a thought, what if? "What if this game of divide and cause chaos is the reason for these attempts? I've wondered why the gunmen never came back to the scene to finish the job and make sure Eric was dead. Are you having some power struggle at Klinger? If anything was leaked to the media, such as the attempts on your lives, wouldn't your Board of Directors demand all of the technology be secured in a place where the company could access it, in case of one of you possibly dying or being taken as a hostage?"

Liam took up the thread of her thoughts. "That way every scrap of technology and all research would be in one place to make it easier to steal." He looked at Darryl. "That's why they want you out of the picture, you must be getting close to the guilty party, and without you, we would be forced to hire a security firm from outside of the company. Your people wouldn't tell them a thing even if you were dead without you leaving standing orders. They would talk to me, but again, the Board will want more say-so in security, and it would be very easy to hire a company by bid, you know what cheap bastards most of them are. Dangle a cut rate slick presentation, and they are like piranha on a wounded water buffalo."

Mackie yawned. It had been a long day, and she needed to sleep. "Guys, I need to go back to the house and get some shuteye. You've given me a lot to think about tonight, and I need to sort it all out in my brain before I decide exactly what I am going to do."

The looks on their faces were priceless. Liam appeared frustrated, Darryl looked disappointed, and John, well John looked resigned. He was shaking his head, and finally said.

"Mackie, what about the words 'bad guys want a hostage or to kill someone' don't you understand? You were seen with Darryl tonight, correct? Tell us, how many times have you been targeted like Darryl has been? And while you're at it, tell us how many times you've been taken as a hostage and tortured in the process. How many times have you been shot, stabbed, confined or whatever, because of your job or association with other people? There's no way you will leave this house until morning. We just found you, and I'm not losing you because you accepted a date."

Liam nodded and Darryl shrugged, "He's right, sugar, you can't leave from here when they saw you enter the pub and disappeared like that. We can take you back in the morning, and no one will think a thing of it."

That reminded her of something she wanted to know. "Speaking of disappearing, how did you know about the passageway between the buildings? That was a slick trick."

John gave her the explanation. "I bought most of the block for investment purposes, it was originally built in the early nineteen hundreds, and used by the boot leggers, and I have been told the brotherhood spent a lot of time in those passageways waiting for the Feds to leave the speakeasy, so they could resume business as usual. There's actually a small room in an off shoot that still has the old chairs and a radio. I left it exactly as I found it because it was such a cool thing to discover. We were exploring and renovating the back rooms of the pub when Liam fell through the wall.

"Incidentally, he fell on his ass and when he told you that he hasn't got any scars, he's lying. The right cheek of his ass was punctured in four spots. It looks like a thick toothed Vampire bit him on the ass."

She couldn't believe he said that with a straight face. "A thick toothed Vampire? Really? So he has dimples on his butt? I bet that's cute in the locker room." She laughed, she couldn't help herself, and looked toward Liam, who was in turn glaring at John.

"Guys, I appreciate your concern, I really do, but I'm a big girl, and can take care of myself. If Dorian shot the intruder, won't they decide that you are expecting trouble, so wouldn't they back up and regroup?"

Again John was shaking his head, and Darryl closed his eyes, and his head went back with his face toward the ceiling. John stood and walked over to where she sat. "Come on, let's get you situated in a bedroom, and we'll all take you back in the morning."

She gave in and followed him through the house and up an ornate wooden staircase. There was a door at the top of the staircase that had a sign "Water Closet" and she smiled at the old-fashioned touches that had been left in the beautiful old home. The original lamps hanging on the wall lighting the corridor had been electrified, and low wattage bulbs caused the old-fashioned yellow glow on the dark wooden paneling. There was a flowered runner down the hallway with beautiful hardwood showing on the sides, and the doorknobs were gilded brass. She loved it.

"You have a beautiful home. I love the old-fashioned elements that you have kept, so many people nowadays would have torn out the paneling and ruined the beauty and craftsmanship of an era when quality was valued."

John smiled and opened the door next to him. "This will be your room, and I hope you like it." The room was large as far as modern bedrooms would go. The bed was huge, brass with porcelain balls breaking the shiny surface. The old wooden dressers and free standing dress closets gave her a case of envy that she'd never owned such a home to house beautiful objects like them.

John interrupted her thoughts. "We converted the fireplaces in each room from coal to natural gas, and through here," he opened a smaller door, "is a shared bathroom with the room next door. It isn't fancy, but we tried to keep the period as true as possible.

He approached her and took her hands in his. "I know it's a lot for you to take in, the inadvertent way that we put your life with ours, the fact that we find you beautiful and sexy enough to make us all agree on convincing you to complete our family." He raised one hand and ran his fingers slowly from her jaw to her ear, and filtered his splayed fingers through her hair.

His palm held her cheek and she felt herself leaning toward him. She gave into the impulse and laid her lips over his. He let her initiate the kiss and took over when her tongue retreated from his lip. His tongue slid over hers and he sucked on her tongue with a rough moan. She pulled back, and he didn't force the issue, but the way he stared into her eyes with longing made her step back another step.

"Thank you for letting me stay, I love your house, and," she raised her hand to her lips. There was no graceful way to tell a man who had just kissed her that she wanted to lie down on that bed and pull him on top of her. She did what any self preserving woman would do, she turned and walked into the bathroom. Instead, she said to him, "Goodnight, John," as she shut the door and leaned against it with her head lowered.

Dammit, Mackie, you are acting so out of character that it isn't funny. What the hell? Are you really thinking about their proposition? Are you nuts? She continued to think about the men and the things they'd said tonight. The conspiracy threat to the Klinger Corporation took a back seat to the personal aspect of the clusterfuck that had started out as a simple dinner date.

She was too tired to worry about it tonight, she would deal with it in the morning. Falling asleep with pictures of three handsome men in her head wasn't a bad thing. The thought caused a smile as she adjusted in the bed and closed her eyes.

John went back to the guys and looked at the time. It was after midnight, and they would have to get up early.

Darryl hadn't put his ruined shirt on, there was no reason to. He was comfortable in his skin, and John crossed over to him while Liam checked his messages. The three of them had been together for eight years, and John was comforted as Darryl's long arms pulled him close when he came near enough for the big guy to embrace.

Darryl had a habit of reading his friend's moods, and he knew John needed reassurance that things would work out for them. "Look, I know that your guts are twisting right now, hell, look at me. How many times have you seen me do a striptease for anyone? She was so worried and focused on her scars that I didn't even think about it. The next thing I know I'm standing there, almost bare assed, so she could see that scars aren't what make you love a person or not. As I stood there, I finally accepted my own fears, and you and Liam, you have no idea how much I love you guys."

He tightened his embrace and leaned in for a deep kiss with John's willing lips. He needed that reassurance himself, and got it from his friend who was closer to him than any blooded brother could be. John's hands ran the length of his spine and over the scars that had once made him avoid mirrors and taking his shirt off, even during sex.

John was in the mood for more than reassurance, it had been days since they'd been together like this and he wanted to taste every inch of Darryl's muscle bound body. He broke the kiss and stayed close as he licked his way over his jaw and down his neck. Licking his way down to the beaded nipple closest to his lips, he nibbled on the small knot before running his hand over its counterpart, and trailing down in a straight line to Darryl's thick cock straining against the zipper of his pants.

He felt his own shirt being pulled from his waistband and knew Liam had decided to leave his messages and join them. He had to back off the expanse of skin long enough to help get the shirt over his head, and went right back to freeing the object of his desire from the material that held Darryl's cock from his eyes. Once he had released the outer layer, he licked his lips at the sight of Darryl's cock behind the thin material of his boxer briefs. He ran his fingertips from nuts to the tip of where his cock ended and had left a small wet spot from pre-cum. He took the waistband of the underwear between his teeth and began to pull it down, revealing just the thick head, and groaned. His teeth let the cloth loose and he licked at the dark pink flesh. He could taste the small droplets that still leaked from Darryl's dick. He reached both hands up and finished pulling the boxers from his lover's hips, dragging them down to his ankles. He ran his hands from the backs of those sculpted thighs to his ass cheeks and squeezed a cheek in each hand. He breathed his words of praise over the big man's dampening skin. "You have the hottest fucking body I've ever seen and seeing you like this makes me want you more each time I have you. So fucking good, you have no idea." His tongue was busy after the last word came out in a strangled groan.

Liam wasn't about to be left out of the play tonight. They hadn't had much time together lately, and this was the perfect opportunity to enjoy each other again. John was on his knees, bent over to enjoy Darryl's cock with his mouth, and seeing them like that with Darryl nude and standing tall and proud was hot. The man was sexy as hell, and while he might consider them sexy, Darryl had them hands down, that was one of the things Liam loved about the man. He wasn't stuck on himself and he was easy to love.

Darryl and John were the best thing that happened to him, and thinking of adding Mackie to their family, well they could only hope she would give the idea serious thought and be open minded enough, no, not open minded so much as open hearted enough to have the capacity to love the three of them.

He crossed over to the smallest drawer of John's desk and grabbed a bottle of lube before kicking his shoes off and removing the rest of his clothes. John was busy, but helped him when he crossed the room and began pulling the shirt of John's body.

He reached around and unsnapped and unbuckled John's pants, pulling them down over his nice ass. He ran his hands over John's back and thighs several times before running lubed fingers along the seam of his ass. With his pants wadded up at the knees, there wasn't much room for having him spread his legs, but Liam sent his fingers to the small hole he was planning on burying his cock inside of. He poured more lube at the top of the seam of his ass and slid two fingers into the warm tight hole.

"Damn, man, you are tight as ever, I can't hardly wait to fuck you. Let me know when you're ready, because I'm too hard to play nice. Seeing you and Darryl is inspiring, you know. Fuck me if it isn't."

He fingered and widened the tight spot and watched as John took half of Darryl's cock into his mouth, pull back, and swallow the thick cock even deeper. He heard John groan as he added a third finger and continued to work his digits as deeply as possible.

When John pushed back on his fingers for the forth time, Liam pulled them from the heated entrance and set the head of his cock to the tight ring that would squeeze the cum from his balls in an embarrassingly short time. He reached down and fondled John's cock and rolled the tight sac of his testicles in his fingers. He held his hip and slowly slid his cock inside of his friend's asshole. He took the shaft of John's cock in his hand and each pump of his hips cause him to jack him off as all three men groaned and moaned their way into a faster pace.

Darryl looked up and saw Mackie standing at the door. He smiled at her and raised his hand in a come join us gesture. She was staring at the three of them with interest and unless he missed his guess, heat. She shook her head when she saw him gesture toward her, but he tried again, and her feet came into the room.

"Come closer, sugar, we won't bite unless you ask us to." She came within three feet of where he was standing and by then, the other men had noticed she was there.

John kept sucking the thick cock in his mouth, holding onto Darryl's ass as he moaned when Liam sank fully into his ass.

Darryl held out his hand toward Mackie and she stepped closer. He reached for her shoulder to bring her closer, and she was so busy watching the two men on the floor that she allowed herself to be brought snug to the side of his body. He bent his head to kiss her under her ear and place small nibbles over her jawline. When he reached her lips, his tongue teased her top lip to open it and once she did, he sent his tongue inside of her mouth and explored every crevice while she moved her tongue along side of his in a gentler but no less carnal kiss.

Mackie had found a t-shirt and a pair of boxers on the bed when she came out of the bathroom John must have been kind enough to provide. Once she'd laid down to sleep, it occurred to her that she'd left her purse with her cell phone inside downstairs. She might have taken the night off, but Laura Downs would demand that she be called in case of any emergency.

She was happy to hear sounds coming from the room that her purse had been left in. She turned the doorknob and stopped in her tracks. When the men had told her that they were exclusive bi-sexual lovers, she hadn't thought much about it at the time. She had seen men having sex before, but none of the men she had seen before looked like these men. Not to mention she had no intention of considering what they appeared to be asking from her then.

Seeing them all naked and caressing each other, kissing and running their hands over all of that muscle was the sexiest thing she could remember seeing. Watching John sucking Darryl's big cock made her body warm, and seeing the look on Liam's face as he sank his cock deep into the doctor's body had made her pussy feel swollen and needy. She could feel the way her nipples beaded into tight knots too.

When Darryl noticed her standing at the door and waved her to him, she almost ran back to her room. The temptation to see these beautiful men making love to each other was too much for her to walk away from, and she drifted closer and closer until Darryl's strong arm encircled her and his lips claimed her own.

He turned her around and put his lips close to her ear. "Watch the two of them, have you ever seen such beautiful people giving each other so much pleasure? The feeling of John's mouth on my cock combined with the taste of your lips has me ready to come. Are you wet? Is your little pussy drenching those boxers?"

His lips opened and his tongue licked at her earlobe and down her neck to her shoulder. "Tell me, sugar, when I put my hand inside the waistband of these shorts, will your pussy enjoy my fingers giving you pleasure?" He wasn't teasing, his hand slid down until his fingers were tickling the small patch of hair she kept neatly trimmed, and ventured further down to rub over the lips of her pussy. His fingers slid in between her slit and his thumb began rubbing back and forth over her clit. Two fingers slipped inside of her cunt and she groaned through her teeth.

"I can feel how wet you are, how about if I do this?" He hooked his two fingers side by side and lifted up, while his thumb pressed down on her clit harder. His other hand reached around and held her breast with the nipple being pinched between his finger and thumb.

"I'm about to come, sugar, how about you join me, and we can watch Liam lose his mind fucking John's asshole while we do it. I know I'd rather be licking your pussy when I come, but until you decide what you want, this will have to do. Can you imagine how it would feel to have the three of us feasting on your sweet flesh? I can, and yeah, sugar, now is a good time to come, come on, baby, give me all that sweetness."

His hips were moving and his hold on her breast tightened, causing a thrill to run through her pussy, and she stiffened, she was coming, and the sensations filling her could no longer be contained without screaming low and panting, as she pumped her hips while her pussy clenched over his fingers.

Liam watched her face as she came and he started to feel his own orgasm begin. He tightened his hand over John's dick, and gave it a few hard pumps before feeling the beautiful cock in his hand swell and begin pulsating as the carpet beneath them became wet from John's sperm soaking it. His own cum shot from his cock, filling the tight dark tunnel of John's ass. He laid over John and ran his hands over the doctor's back and thighs repeatedly. He could feel his cock shrinking from John's body, and he groaned again once the sensitized flesh of his cock pulled free.

Chapter 10

Mackie laid on the bed again, she needed sleep, and she needed to think. Why she was acting out of character baffled her. She had never in her wildest imagination thought there might be a remote possibility that she could end up in this situation. One man had been an old dream and goal. Two men were strictly fantasy and reading preference, but three men?

Yes, yes, yes… hold on, girlie, you need to think this through. It's not like you're doing a job here, it's not as easy as that. The only person she would need to protect would be herself. Yet allowing her emotions to get involved with these men would require more bravery than she was certain she possessed. She fell asleep with the pictures of the beautiful naked men she'd left downstairs when she panicked and all but ran from the room.

It seemed that she'd just drifted off to sleep when there was a knock on the bedroom door, and Dorian came into the room without her saying a word. She was still under the covers with her head buried under the pillow.

The pillow was pulled off her head and she opened one eye to see the man's chest. She turned her head and saw that he was smiling and had a small tray with coffee and a bagel sitting on the nightstand waiting for her.

"Okay, if this is a peace offering, I accept and grovel for forgiveness for my part yesterday." She sat up, keeping the sheet from falling away from her thighs. Dorian shook his head at her words and told her on his way back through the door.

"Time to get up, lady, the men will meet you downstairs in twenty minutes."

Mackie had the cup of coffee to her lips within seconds of the door closing behind him. The bagel was toasted just right and she enjoyed crunching the warm bread as she thought about her day to come.

She felt awkward wearing a dress without panties, but hers were a mess, and she left them rinsed out and hanging on the shower bar. She hadn't remembered to grab her purse last night and was concerned about that too. She never forgot to take her phone to bed with her. This situation had her feeling so off kilter and confused that she began questioning her sanity. Being honest with her self, she admitted to feeling restless for months, and now she had an inkling why.

The minute she saw the three men standing at the bottom of the stairs, she knew in her gut that she wasn't going to be able to ignore what they'd done together and shared with her. Thankfully they had been smart enough not to push her when she left the room early this morning. They wanted her to know what she was getting into if she decided to give the unusual relationship a chance. Fuck.

John was dressed in a light blue button up shirt and black slacks. Liam looked like he stepped out of a magazine in his business suit, and Darryl looked like a wet dream in his leather jacket and muscle shirt over jeans and boots. They all turned to watch her step off the bottom stair.

She had to smile, they looked so anxious and hopeful that, what? Were they afraid that she would be embarrassed or mad? Her smile must have reassured them because she could almost feel the way their shoulders relaxed when they saw her.

"Good morning, guys, you all look handsome and ready for the day. Who's taking me home?" She looked at Darryl and shook her head. "I am not riding on a bike in this dress, so if that was the plan forget it." He grinned and wiggled his eyebrows, but shook his head no. "I need to get my purse, and I will be right with you." She headed to the den, but Liam stopped her in her tracks by saying.

"Your purse is right here, I figured you might want it, I know how women and their purses are. Remind me to tell you about my mother's collection of handbags. She drives everyone crazy when she misplaces hers."

Mackie bit her lip because the other men laughed outright at his statement. Whatever the story about his mother was, it must be a good one. "Thank you, but I only carry one when I have no other option." She waved a hand indicating the dress she wore. "No pockets, to put things."

John looked at his watch. "We need to get moving, I have an appointment with Mike this morning and he gets pissy when his schedule is thrown off." He stepped closer to Mackie and took her hand in his, before walking them to the back door of the house.

The garage was attached to the house, and the SUV was silver with dark tinted windows. There was a silver blue sports car next to it, but they all piled into the SUV with Darryl driving.

John was the first to be dropped off at his research facility. He leaned over and gave Mackie a open mouth kiss on her lips that had her hands reaching for his shoulders, before breaking the kiss and exiting the vehicle. Darryl waited until he'd entered the building before leaving the parking lot.

She felt the mood shift as he had walked into the open between the SUV and the building. "So why don't you tell me the rest of the story here while we are en route to the Senator's house? I can see you're concerned John got inside the building, and I could see the way you watched for threats. Has someone been taking potshots at you guys too? I mean aside from the house being broken into and the problem at the pub last night. This is more than just a jealous co-worker, and more than you are telling me, so how about sharing here?"

Liam took her hand in his and examined her fingers before answering, "John's research has just been awarded a huge amount of money to continue the search for antidotes and vaccines against the newest chemical threats that some countries are threatening to use to start wars. The country's power people threaten to use chemicals if other countries refuse to sell or give them conventional weapons to maintain their armies. Making their threats useless with his research would screw up their blackmailing abilities, and they would have nothing to threaten with. No one was supposed to know what company was close to finding the answers, yet somehow John has been outed and it had to have come from the same source that leaked the Drone Tech advancement. John is the brains behind the research, take him out, and the project is shut down.

"Once he enters the building, he doesn't leave for any reason unless he has at least two of Darryl's men with him. We know he's feeling restless because of the confinement. Thankfully, last night helped him release some of the stress. Being as independent and normally capable of taking care of his own safety makes it hard to deal with what he considers babysitters."

He raised her hand to his mouth and kissed the back of it, lingering long enough to touch his tongue where he'd placed the kiss, and kissed it again. It was the oddest thing, but it also was a sexy thing for him to do. Mackie wanted to, hell, she didn't know exactly what she wanted to do. These men confused her.

Darryl parked in front of a small mini mall and left the motor running when he got out and headed into the chain store coffee shop.

She turned to watch him walk inside of the building, scanning the area as much as possible, given the fact that she was in the back seat and Liam was obstructing part of the view. "If I'd known he was going to stop, I would have asked him to grab me a Frappe, I love the things way too much."

Liam smiled and pulled her from her seat onto his lap and kissed her neck. "Well, if he doesn't bring out what you like, we can send him back for the right thing." He kissed her neck again and ran his hand up and down her thigh while talking. "I woke up this morning wanting you. My cock was so hard that it took maybe three minutes in the shower this morning to cum just imagining your beautiful lips wrapped around the damn thing. Every time you are near, I have to start doing math in my head, or I would be crawling after you, begging you to take pity on me and allow me to make love to you."

He shook his head, "I don't act like this, I never see a woman that I'd do anything to get her to smile at me, since maybe high school. Yet, the first time I saw you standing there, ready and willing to shoot me, I stood there like a dumbass, and all I could do was stare. My fuck up caused you to be shot, and it has haunted me since that day."

More kisses and tiny licks with his tongue followed her jawline. "I'm such a sick fuck that when John and I undressed you, at first, all I could think about was sucking your nipple into my mouth, and if you hadn't been bleeding so badly I might have done it. I saw the scars and I wanted to trace each one with my fingers, my lips, tongue, whatever way there was to touch you."

He pulled his head back and sighed. "Like I said, I don't allow myself to be controlled by beautiful women, but all I've wanted to do is wallow in and on you since the first time I saw you. I want to know everything about you, where you come from, what's your favorite color, do you like chocolate or flowers? The things I want to know are endless, but this need to have you involves your enthusiasm too. I need you to want me as badly as I crave you.

"I know that didn't make a lot of sense, and I know that this has been an overwhelming twenty hours. I've had months to think about you, and fantasize about you joining me, Darryl, and John, to solidify our family." He kissed her lips gently and set her back in her seat. "All I ask is that you think about it, think about being the center of our lives, think about loving arms holding you at night, every night. Can you do that?"

She nodded her head and sat back in her seat. "I can't promise anything at this point. I won't lie to you, I have thought about you men over the months, but it never occurred to me the three of you were together, and no matter what some of the books I've read say. People don't have relationships like the one that you men are asking me to be a part of. I was happy when you called, and I was looking forward to seeing you again, talking, maybe swapping stories and hearing how Eric and Jenny were doing. I've been in some very tight situations, but last night was one of the more unusual dates in recent memory.

"I don't have answers, or even have an idea here. You say John is used to being independent, I think our past history is a good example of my nature. I don't let men manhandle me unless I want them to. I'm not a docile doormat, but for some reason, I feel comfortable with you all." She looked out of the window toward the coffee shop door for Darryl to come back to them.

She didn't see him, so she turned back to Liam. "Seeing the three of you last night was the most beautiful thing I've seen. The caring and tenderness about brought me to tears. That's something else I never do, I don't cry. The only relationships I've had are a few passing lust filled nights. I don't do love and commitment, and now in one night everything has changed. I'm not sure I can handle it. I'm attracted, I admit it, but can I give you a commitment?" She shook her head. "I don't know you. All I know is what I could glean from public records and a few other resources. The only promise I will make is that I will think about it, and If Laura Downs releases me from her employment on good terms, I'll help you ferret out your rat."

Liam smiled, and her body tingled seeing that smile, he was flirting with her and she smiled back, that smile, yeah, she was sunk and knew it, but she would still take her time to make certain this is what she wanted.

Darryl finally left the store, and in his hands was a short sided cardboard carton with several bags sitting upright in the box. Liam unlocked the door and took the box from him so Darryl could get in the driver's seat.

Darryl looked into the back of the vehicle where Mackie was sitting and grinned. "You get a special treat this morning, not what I would have liked to give you, but it will have to do for now. No peeking until we get to the house."

He reversed the SUV and they were on their way to take her home.

Mackie let the men into the house and led them through the formal sitting room and into the kitchen through the dining room. The house was a rental for the last year of Laura and Thom's time in the area, so the furnishings belonged to the landlord. Mackie knew that Laura cringed every time she saw the ornate dining room furniture, and knew the woman hated the formal setting in every room but the kitchen. Laura loved to cook when she had the time. They found the couple sitting in the sunroom talking while Laura arranged a vase of beautiful spring daffodils.

Thom was wearing his sweats, and Mackie knew the man kept his muscles in good shape by working out every morning, so they must not have been awake very long.

Laura saw her first and grinned. "Are you going to ask me if you can keep them? Usually it is puppies or kittens that follow you home. I see that you have upgraded to men." She laughed as Mackie turned pink cheeked and crossed over to the three people, holding out her hand to greet the strangers.

Mackie made the introductions and Thom Hurrell walked over to invite them to sit down and rest for a while.

Feeling woefully underdressed, she excused herself to go change. "I'll be right back, I need to take care of something."

No one was paying attention to her, Darryl was distributing the goodies that he'd purchased at the coffee shop and Laura was clapping her hands at the sight of the double caramel mocha frappe smothered in whipped cream that he held out for her to take. Liam handed over a large black coffee to Thom, and was opening a bag filled with biscotti and cream filled snacks.

She had no idea that both men watched her as she exited the room, but the married couple noticed, and Thom gave a small shake of his head toward his matchmaking wife. She was positively beaming and gushing over the thoughtful gesture they had brought with them.

When everyone was seated, Thom looked directly at Liam and asked him. "Now the niceties have been observed, and we've been sweetened up, how about telling us what's going on? The last time I saw either of you the circumstances were a bit different. By the way, thank you for not shooting my wife's bodyguard this time. She gets upset when that happens." He watched the scowls and enjoyed making the men uncomfortable. He sat back and waited for Liam to tell them what was going on.

Liam nodded, he acknowledged the dig about shooting Mackie, and started retelling the story of the traitor in the midst of Klinger Corporation.

Ten minutes into the story, where the subject of his date with Mackie came up, Laura excused herself. Men saw things much differently than women did, and she wanted to get Mackie's part firsthand. Liam Klinger was leaving things out of his story, she would bet on it, and unless she missed her guess, it involved the two handsome men that were still entertaining Thom with the story of intrigue.

Mackie finished blow drying her hair and contemplated having it cut. It took forever to deal with each morning and she liked it long, but maybe a shorter cut would save time. She was still pondering the idea when she exited the bathroom and came to a stop once she noticed Laura sitting on the old blanket chest at the foot of her bed. "Oh I'm sorry it took so long for me to get changed, was there something you needed?"

Laura shook her head and smiled. "No, I came up here to get your story. Those two walking wet dreams are still brainstorming with Thom downstairs. I want to hear what you have to say about last night." She grinned, "And don't stand there and tell me that nothing happened, when you left the room, I swear both of them watched you like you were a steak and they were starving Rottweiler's. My mouth went dry the minute they smiled. You know it's a good thing Thom took care of me this morning or I might have jumped on one of them myself. Tell me, are they as good as they appear to be?"

Mackie laughed a little and shook her head. "You have no idea, I swear I don't, I, how to describe last night. Yes, they are all extraordinary, and I haven't had, well, damn." She took a deep breath and sat down next to her employer and best friend.

"You know how we did some background on Liam, Darryl, and John?" She got a nodded response, and shrugged. "Well there were a few things that weren't in the files that we accessed about them. They are close, and by close, I mean as close as men can get, but that's not the part that is making me stutter like this. They have decided that they want me." She raised her hands and dropped them back onto her lap. "All three of them. They want me to be, I don't know what I would call it. Last night was the most beautiful thing I've ever seen and done, but I don't know how we could make something like that work. I'm used to being different, independent and strong, but one look and they make me wish I could be more."

Laura put her arm around Mackie's shoulders and they sat that way for a few minutes. When she started talking Mackie was surprised, not as shocked as she probably should be, but it was no longer a mystery why Ishmeal was treated like family.

"I have never told another soul this, and you might be surprised to know that Thom and I have a third in our bed at times. Ishy is loved by both of us, and we would never hurt him. For obvious reasons, he cannot live here, and we will never be able to go public as a ménage relationship, but he's been with us since a year after our marriage over twenty-five years ago. When I retire at the end of my term this year, Thom will retire the following year and Ishy will retire at the same time or within a few months. You know that we own that farm up in the Detroit area right? The house is huge, and the housekeeper will not be a live-in."

Laura looked in Mackie's widened eyes and smiled, "Our middle son, Wyatt, is fathered by Ishy, and he knows it. After three days of sulking, he managed to come to terms with knowing about the three of us, and he still carries his father's name in a way. His middle name is Ishmeal." She gave Mackie another squeeze and let her go, before standing. "You have the attraction, and men like that would never take a chance telling someone what they have shared with you, unless they were sincerely interested. They have far more to lose than you do, yet they still opened a vein and gave you information that would destroy them publically if it got out to the wrong people.

"Liam Klinger told us that you were brought into the trap last night without your knowledge or consent, regardless of how you became involved, you have my blessing and love. If you decide to stay with me, we'll weather the controversy of you being seen with Darryl Reynolds. If you decide to go with them, I'll be happy for you, and enjoy knowing that you will have finally found someone to love you, even three someones."

She brushed her hand down the back of Mackie's hair and said, "You deserve to be happy, you deserve to be loved and have someone for you to know you can depend on to take care of you, just as much as you will take care of them. Don't let fear hold you back, if you want them now, love will grow as long as you are all honest with each other."

Laura left her still sitting on the chest, and Mackie digested everything she'd heard as she dropped the bath sheet and got dressed for the day. Would it be as easy or as simple as honesty? Could she find the love and compassion inside of herself to love three men equally? She was thirty years old, and had been solitary most of her life, taking care of others was what she did. The occasional wish for someone of her own was being handed to her, and she was almost afraid to take it.

She was still arguing the pros and cons of her choice when she came downstairs and handed Darryl her suitcase and gave Liam her old Army duffel bag that was packed to capacity. She walked back to the stairs and picked up her backpack and the cat carrier. GreyC was going with her on this new adventure.

Thom and Laura waved goodbye from the front door, and for some reason Mackie choked up. She looked at Darryl and Liam in turn and wondered, *what have they done to me*?

Chapter 11

They dropped Liam off at his office, and again, Darryl waited until he was safely inside the big glass doors before continuing on their way. They drove for almost half an hour before she asked where they were heading. "I don't recognize the area, or I wouldn't ask."

Darryl gave her a quick side glance and grinned. "First, I'm taking you to the main house, and after we drop your bags off and change into something more comfortable, I thought we could enjoy the rest of the day entertaining each other."

She turned her head to look out of the side glass. He was grinning too much for her to be at ease right now. "What exactly do you mean by that? What kind of entertaining are you planning?"

He laughed outright and just shook his head. By the time they pulled into the long driveway and stopped the SUV in front of an old farmhouse, she was nervous. Darryl grabbed the duffle and the suitcase when she reached for it, so she was left with the backpack and cat carrier. "You know, I'm not exactly helpless, right? I'm used to carrying my things, and pulling my weight. I appreciate your help, but you don't have to coddle me."

He transferred the suitcase to the same hand that had the duffle slung over the shoulder, and punched in a series of numbers on the keypad, it clicked the lock, but when she tried to turn the handle, it refused to open. He laid his hand straight on the metal panel, and the door swung open.

"Oh that's a nice trick there," Mackie complimented the secondary locking system that only the owner or someone who's print was programed into the reader could gain access into the house. "I haven't seen this one on the market, is it one of your designs?"

He led her through the house and up the steep stairs. "Yes, I'm not the genius that John is, or the slick business ace that Liam is, but I have brains, and I like to tinker a bit here and there."

They stopped outside the third door in the hallway and she turned the knob and stepped inside. This room was modern compared to the house in town, and she liked it, but there was no character in the furnishings, and everything in the room appeared to be reproduction pieces of good quality, but 1950's blonde wood and squared edges. It would do to start.

Darryl told her to worry about unpacking later. "We have things to do, so bust out a pair of your oldest jeans and a sweatshirt or t-shirt and a sweater that you don't have sentimental attachments to. Sturdy shoes and you will want long sox on too." He looked at his watch and frowned. "The sooner we get moving the better, I'll meet you downstairs in ten." He dropped her luggage on the bed and left the room before she could question him.

GreyC was napping in her carrier and there was plenty of food and water in the side cups that were built in inside of the thing, so she would be fine for a while longer. So she left the carrier on the floor by the bed, and opened the duffle. She didn't have any old clothing, everything she might have possessed had been blown up with her house. She pulled on jeans and a t-shirt and added a zippered hoodie. She had hiking boots, and hoped they would be good enough for what he planned for the day. She pulled her hair up onto a high ponytail and braided it. It wasn't the prettiest hairdo, but it would keep strands from getting in her line of sight if they were going to the range. She checked her watch and headed out to meet Darryl downstairs.

He was waiting for her and nodded in appreciation for her outfit. "You look beautiful no matter what you're wearing, and I'm glad that you have boots, you'll need them, let's go."

He led them to the hip-roofed barn and still managed to hold the door for her before she could open it for herself. They went through the common area that housed two large tractors and several horse stalls and the hayloft appeared to be half full of fragrant alfalfa. She didn't ask questions because she was busy scoping the place out for possible future use. They came to a double door near the rear of the barn and again Darryl punched in buttons and his hand slapped the panel. The door opened and he stood back for her to go through first. This polite treatment was driving her crazy, but she smiled a little and walked into a room full of guns and knives, swords, bows and arrows. And she was itching to touch each and every article.

She grinned and looked at Darryl as he stood just inside the door watching her and her reaction to his playroom. He shut the door behind him and walked over to a display of handguns. He smiled at her and wiggled his eyebrows.

"Hey, little girl, wanna play with me?" He waved his hand across the span of the collection and she almost ran over to his side. "If we play for an hour and you can stand the company, then we venture further afield. Do you have any idea of how difficult it is to find a date that likes to play with my toys? I took a date to a gun range and it turned into a disaster. She whined about the noise and the smell of gunpowder, and to top that off, she almost shot me. It was embarrassing." He selected a .38 special and raised an eyebrow when she zeroed in on the hammerless version of the same .38 he held.

"You can choose what ever you want to shoot, I try to change guns each time I come in here so I keep accurate with all of them, it's also a good excuse to clean them after I use them, so none of them get dusty or rust when it's damp outside. If you look under the benches you will see bins of litter and silica. It sucks the water out of the air, and I keep fans going all the time for airflow, and it works for now. When I get the new building finished, I won't have to worry about any of that. The room will be controlled electronically." He grabbed two boxes of bullets and walked to the blank wall with a single door. "Come on, you're gonna love this."

Mackie was delighted to see that he guessed right, she loved his underground setup. "How did you do this? I love it, but how did you manage to do all of this?"

The "this" she spoke of was a shooting range complete with doors with cardboard bad guys behind them and a few innocents. She shot a bad guy that was hiding behind a plastic shrub and almost shot a little kid silhouette peeking over a windowsill. They spent over an hour talking and shooting.

Darryl explained how he designed and made the place his own. "We bought the place for somewhere to unwind and enjoy getting out of the fishbowl of everyday life. There was four silage pits already dug into the ground next to the barn, and I knew the farm would never use them again, so I brought in a contractor and we drew up the designs for an underground range. It was fun trying to find a good concrete man to pour the curved walls and flat floor, but I love it."

They were on the way back to the gun room when Mackie stopped in her tracks and stared at his back as he kept walking, until he noticed she wasn't following him. He retraced his steps and stopped in front of her. "What's wrong? Are you okay?"

She blurted the first thing that came to her mind. "You're DE Fields, aren't you? I feel a little dumb here, but in my defense, I never thought about it until now." The security gadget company was relatively new on the market, and she'd purchased some of their offerings for the setup of her home in the country.

He shook his head no, and sighed. "No, my father is DE Fields, I am just Darryl Fielding. I do hold several patents, and some may be sold in the stores, but you can be sure the old man doesn't know who invented those items, or he wouldn't carry them." He began walking and she followed without further conversation.

Once they reached the gun room, Darryl pulled down a springboard table and took a cleaning kit from the shelf in the wall behind where the board had been hanging on the wall on its hinges. "I'm sorry, I never talk about my old man. Long story short, I came home on leave, found my mother dying in a hospital bed, and my father and her nurse fucking in the spare bedroom. The whore was wearing my mother's jewelry and her fur coat while his old ass was drilling her cunt." He shoved the cleaning rod into the barrel of the revolver and continued cleaning while he finished his story.

"The house was willed to me through my mother's parents. My mother was gasping for every breath because that cunt hadn't turned the oxygen on, and they were making a joke of her last minutes on earth. I beat his ass and tossed him out of the house. His whore was screaming and threatening to call the cops, I made her leave my mother's jewelry on the fucking bed, watched as she grabbed her clothes, and locked the door behind her." He finished wiping the pistol down with a soft cloth and set it in the designated spot. "DE tried to get back into the house, but if he'd succeeded, I would have killed him. He tried to have me arrested, but by the time the police he'd called showed up, the paramedics were hauling my mother's body out of the house, and I was not in the mood for his excuses. I let the cops stay while he packed his shit, and left in his fancy little pussy trap sports car.

"I told the cops what he and his whore were doing when I walked in, I wanted them charged with negligence and anything else that could be used to put them away. The only thing that kept them from being arrested was that my mother was terminally ill with brain cancer that had spread into her bones. She only had a few days left, according to her doctors. He ended up marrying the slut three months after my mother died. She divorced him after three years and the two kids they had are now teenagers, and I hope they're giving that bastard hell." He took the pistol from her hands, looked it over, and put it with the others.

"If he had waited a few weeks, she would have been gone, and I might not have liked him playing around so soon after mom's death, but I would've probably let it pass after a while. The lack of respect he had for the woman he'd been married to for twenty-five years sickened me. He was never much of a father figure, always claiming he had work to do, and we believed him. Now I know that he married my mother for her family's money. It's how he financed the first DE Fields store.

"My mother must have known ten years before her death, because she changed her will. His debt to her for financing his store was forgiven at her death, but that is all he received. It was quite a surprise when the will was read. I got what was left, and the man even tried to swindle me out of my inheritance two years after she passed."

Darryl gave her a sad smile. "I'm sorry to unload on you like this, he really is a selfish bastard, and isn't worth thinking about."

Mackie reached out and pulled his hand into hers. "I need a hug, and you need a hug too. We can't pick our parents or relatives, all you can do is smile and nod your head as you keep walking past. Someday I might unload on you about my history, trust me, it's not nearly as interesting as yours is."

They held each other for a few minutes, Mackie wanted to ease his pain filled memories, but she had no experience in helping anyone with grief. She had never allowed anyone to get close enough for her to care about that much to feel pain when they died. Laura and Thom were the exception, but that connection took place over years, and now, what was she getting herself into? The urge to track down DE Fielding and hurt him was strong, but it was the only thing she could think of that might ease Darryl's pain. She knew nothing would restore his mother to life, but to know that your own father was such an evil fucker had to hurt. She made the offer just to cheer him up, but if he said "Sure, go ahead and do it," she knew she would.

"Would you like me to track him down and castrate him? I could break both of his legs and maybe break his back and put him in a wheelchair for the rest of his life. We could lock him in an efficiency apartment with his favorite nurse and see if they enjoy getting to know one another again." She pulled her head back from his shoulder to see his face while she tried to get him to smile. *Or, I have an even better idea.*

"I have a few inventions of my own, why don't we open a new company and run him out of business? I have financing, and you know what you are doing businesswise, or get Liam to help you."

She grinned, her head filling with the idea, and thinking which of her inventions would be useful to sell to security companies.

Darryl laughed out loud then he pulled her into his arms for a deep kiss, and his hands wandered during the moments that his mouth was locked onto hers. When they came up for air, he pushed the hair back from her temple. "Thanks, sugar, but you don't need to do any of that. Although I do want to hear about these inventions of yours. The morning that we met and through the evening, I was green with jealousy over some of your toys. That electric gridding was impressive. Not to mention the bunker, that place is great. Someday you need to tell me about the rest too. My guess is you had some high profile people down there and you acted as a decoy for the bad guys."

She shook her head, "You know I can't talk about my work, all I will say is that you are very observant, and we can leave it at that."

He nodded and took her hand again. "Fair enough, so how about we have some real fun now?"

They left the gun room and went outside to the garage. There were five quad runners that obviously were frequently put into service. Scratches and dents riddled the plastic and metal bodies of the small vehicles. "Here we go, grab a helmet from the wall and pick a weapon, the paintballs are loaded and ready to use, so if you're not familiar with them be careful."

They played in the muddy fields for a couple of hours shooting at targets and running the little quads up and down manmade hills and muddy tracks. She laughed more during their playtime than she could ever remember doing in her life. When Darryl told her that it was time to head back, she was disappointed.

It didn't occur to her that she was pouting, her bottom lip was sticking out, and Darryl drove his quad closer. "Hey we can come back another day you know, we come out here at least twice a month to blow off stress and just cut loose. I promise, you'll have more days like this one. Now, the last one back to the garage has to buy dinner tonight."

The race back distracted her, and she was laughing as they pulled the quads into their spot. They had to hurry to get dressed in clean clothing to drive back to the city to collect the other two men, and met downstairs when they were ready.

Darryl thanked her for keeping him company for the day and she smiled.

"I should be the one thanking you. I swear I haven't had so much fun in I don't know how long. I really enjoyed goofing off with you today." He reached over the console and took her hand in his for the duration of the drive to pick up John.

John came out of the building with two people hard on his heels and once he entered the SUV, the other people melted into the crowd of people that were beginning to leave the building for the day.

Mackie turned to greet him, and almost bumped noses with him as he leaned forward and kissed her on the cheek, then on her lips.

He drew back too soon for her taste, but his words warmed her.

"Hey, beautiful, and you too, buddy. I needed that kiss. All I've been doing all day is daydreaming and mooning around the lab. If I'd had my car, I would have left hours ago. This restriction on my movement is getting old. You need to catch this piece of shit soon, because I'm going to break the chain one of these days. Especially now that we have a woman for me to impress and spend time with."

Darryl grinned and came back with, "Yeah, and let's not forget her cat. He's at the house too you know."

Mackie grinned and raised her eyebrow, "I'll have you know that GreyC is a lady, and she wouldn't appreciate the two of you not recognizing her importance. She is a premier mouser, and she keeps my shoulders warm when it's cold outside. She also likes the last bite of meat on my plate, and does as she damn well pleases the rest of the time."

The discussion on cats versus dogs carried them until they reached Klinger International. Darryl texted Liam, and they waited for him to reply. After five minutes, Darryl texted him again, and the phone vibrated almost immediately.

"Son of a raggedy assed bitch, Liam says he's hitching a ride with Mason home tonight, something came up, and he can't talk right now." Darryl looked at John, and they both looked at Mackie.

Whatever they were thinking she wanted to know about it. "Okay, so what's with the looks? Do we go in and bring him out the hard way?" She pretended to rub her hands together in excitement, and her clowning did gain her two small smiles, but Darryl and John also shook their heads. "Might as well tell me, or we can sit here all evening. Making GreyC stay in her carrier won't get you points from her, but then you all won't care if she puts a dead mouse or bat on the pillow next to your head in the middle of the night either, will you?"

John spoke, "Mackie, Mason, Liam's grandfather, left for France early this morning. The text was a way to let us know something is wrong."

Darryl nodded his head, and added, "Hitchcock must be the leak. Liam capitalized the word Hitching." He looked at John and shook his head.

"That guy has to be nuts to try his shit here in the building." He looked at Mackie and grinned. "I've got a plan."

Chapter 12

Mackie rode the elevator to the top floor and took the first turn on the left. She entered the door with Liam's name stenciled on it. Her hair was now loose around her shoulders and arms, and she had she her suit jacket in the SUV. Her blouse was unbuttoned to show a nice view of the ample cleavage between her breasts. She used the keycard to open the door that Darryl had given her, and barged into the room without knocking or announcing her presence. She immediately began talking as she entered the room.

"Liam, we have a date, and I don't like to be kept waiting, I'm not one of your bimbos and I, oh, you have company." She stopped talking for a second and continued forward toward the desk where Liam sat, and his father, Drummond, sat in one of the chairs facing the desk while a large man stood off to the side and another stood over Drummond with a pistol pointed at his neck.

She held out her hand to the man without the gun as she moved toward him. "How do you do, I am Maxine, and I'm pleased to meet you, but I need to have Liam come with me because we have dinner reservations and he is meeting with my parents. I'm sure you understand." She cut her eyes to Liam who was looking like he would have a heart attack.

"Daddy is not going to be pleased if you are late again, and you know how he acts when someone upsets his schedule." She cut her gaze back to the big man who had automatically taken her hand and was shaking it.

She smiled and gripped his hand tighter before leaning into his personal space and kneeing him in the crotch. She grabbed his wrist and twisted it while he was off balance, and brought her knee up hard while he was bent over and connected with the man's nose. His scream was nice to hear over the sounds of flesh connecting behind her, but the man she was abusing was tougher than he looked, and he came up swinging. She leaned back out of the way of the fist, and was ready to put her fist into his bloody nose when a large hand on her shoulder pulled her back from the fight, and she heard Drummond tell her to have a seat.

She looked at the elder Klinger, and nodded. She picked up the .22 semi-auto from the floor where she assumed either Drummond or Liam had knocked it from the assailant's hand, and went to the corner nearest the door to stay out of the way of the fighting. Darryl and John came rushing in the door, and stopped as they saw what was happening. Mackie smiled and waved them over to where she stood.

Liam had the gunman on the floor, putting some serious punches to the guy's face and chest. They rolled around on the floor, with each man getting a punch in here and there, but Liam had strength on his side, and it was obvious to the onlookers that he was winning the fight.

Drummond was showing off in Mackie's opinion. She said to her companions, "Ol' boy knows how to fight, he's good with his fists, and moves fast. Look at that, he just broke the guy's rib, did you hear it break?" The pounding he was giving the man was continuing, and she grinned, "Now he's just showing off, that guy won't be moving once he falls down."

John grinned back at her as Darryl went to the door to talk to the three uniformed cops that walked in.

"Dru was always good with his fists, he was a boxer in college, and in the ring, he never lost a fight. He's enjoying himself, look at that smile." John left her side and walked toward where Drummond had his victim against the wall as he continued to pummel his body.

Mackie shook her head and leaned against the wall as the police finally pulled Liam off his opponent, and John talked Drummond into letting his fall where he stood. She didn't hear what he said, but Drummond shook his head and she saw he shook his shoulders and his arms trying to loosen them up. She called it shaking off the adrenalin when it happened to her in the past.

She handed the gun to the officer that came to get her information, and he raised his brow, but left her after his questions had been answered. John came over to her and took her hand.

"Let's go, Darryl and Liam will be taking Dru home, and now that I'm off the leash, Darryl gave me the keys to the SUV. We can stop and grab take-out on the way to the house."

John was in a good mood and when he got into the driver's seat, he pretended to kiss the steering wheel, telling it how he'd missed his baby. "I haven't been allowed to drive on my own for almost a month now, and believe me, I've missed it."

Mackie let him talk, he had a sexy voice, not too low, and not too high, she smiled to herself, his voice was just right. He might be the most compassionate of the three men, but his streak of male ego was as strong. His was just subtler. There was no doubt that he would be as good with his fists as Liam appeared to be, but John was more of the diplomat, at least from what she'd seen of his character so far.

She had to ask him to stop at the closest grocery store, "I need to get a litter pan for GreyC or she'll find a corner. She hates it when she can't dig a hole."

They stopped at a large store and had to park several yards from the front doors of the place because the parking lot was almost filled with vehicles.

John insisted on pushing the cart, and from the way he wanted to go up and down almost every isle in the place, she knew that this was some new adventure for him. "Who normally does your grocery shopping? I get the impression this isn't exactly something you're used to doing."

It took him a little while to answer her and when he did, she grinned.

His, "I am calculating the number of products per aisle and shelf. For instance, the cereal aisle contains eighty-two varieties of product, not including the bins with bags of the same cereal, yet is made cheaper due to the advertising and name branding. The product designated as hot cereal is diverse, yet not as large of a market, or there would be more than ten offerings." He shook his head at the numbers and shrugged his shoulder when he saw her grin. "I find it entertaining, but I don't expect anyone else to understand."

As they made their way down the next aisle, she pointed out the large array of toilet paper and other paper products. "Can you tell how many trees were killed to wipe our butts for the next month or so?" The look she got from him made her laugh out loud and promised retaliation.

They got to the pet supply aisle and she bent to lift a large box of scoopable cat litter, John was scowling at her when she looked up after plopping the heavy box into the cart. "What?" She followed his eyes to the box, and she wondered what the big deal was, did he have something against that particular brand of litter?

He shook his head, but the small talk they'd been indulging in came to a halt. He asked if she needed anything else, and when she shook her head, he headed for the check out lanes. He unloaded the cart, and when the total was rung up, he gave her a very nasty look when she started to hand over her debit card to the amused clerk. His card was shoved toward the woman and Mackie didn't know what his problem was, but from the look on his face she wouldn't have long to find out what his deal was.

By the time they got back to the farmhouse, Mackie was ready to thump him a good one. She tried to make conversation, but his grunts and short clipped replies pissed her off. He handed her the keys and asked her to get the door. She grabbed the keys and did as he asked as he gathered their purchases, then carried them inside.

She went up to the room she'd been given and picked up GreyC's carrier. The cat wasn't happy and hissed at her, but she settled down once they began moving. John had the plastic bin filled halfway to the top with litter and had placed it in the utility room. GreyC gave him a quick glance and jumped into the bin. Mackie was satisfied the little furball would be fine now, and went into the kitchen to begin frying burgers for their dinner. It wasn't gourmet, but it would fill the need and she sliced tomatoes and shredded lettuce to go with the burgers, she snacked on cheese while flipping the meat patties. John disappeared shortly after they'd stepped into the house, but if he was going to continue his pissy attitude, she would take her food into another room to eat. She had everything laid out on the counter and went to the stairs to yell for his attention.

He surprised her by opening a door near the steps, and she could see that it was the door to the basement. Okay, so he hung out in the basement like the mad scientists in cartoons. The thought made her grin, and she went back to the kitchen to build her burger.

The tall sweaty body with arms that encircled her from behind while her hands were full of bun and tomato, held her close long enough for him to snatch the pickle from her plate, and then backed away quickly. She fished another pickle from the jar and added a slice of onion to her sandwich. He was waiting by the table with a cold beer extended toward her, and she smiled.

"Okay, the beer in exchange for a pickle works for me. Help yourself to the food, I made enough for both of us you know. I have basic skills in the kitchen so don't expect me to do all of the cooking." She bit into the bun and closed her eyes, savoring the taste. Her stomach rumbled and John laughed.

"Sugar, you need to feed that tummy, the poor thing is thanking you for the scraps that you send it." He filled his own mouth and sat back in his chair chewing rapidly, and half of the burger was soon gone. "I worked through lunch today, so I'm hungry too." He chewed his way through the rest of the burger and got up to make another one. "You don't have to worry about starving around here, we all can cook some things, and when all else fails, the grill is ready to be put in use. You have heard of the unwritten law that men are born grillers, right? We keep the freezer stocked up with meat, and whoever gets home first starts dinner, or one of us brings something home when we're here." He sat down, and asked, "So tell me something about you, all I know is that you play with some fascinating toys, and that you might be the only female I would bet on to whip Liam's ass in a fight. Don't get me wrong, Darryl and I can deal with just about anything coming our way, but Liam has been trained in self-defense and at least two Asian disciplines of martial arts since he was old enough to walk."

She shook her head, "There's not much to tell really, when I graduated from high school, I saw a posting about female security officers. After looking into the profession a little deeper, I was interested. I took a test, and after the fact decided to apply at the FBI." She shrugged, "I was assigned as a bodyguard for several low profile diplomats, and gradually worked into more significant assignments. That's how I met the General and Senator Downs, I was assigned to her detail, and some radical decided it would be a good idea to shoot a high profile Senator from the USA.

"When I recovered, I decided to try freelancing, and so far it's worked out for me." She noticed that John was picking small pieces of his second burger off, and his hand would drop casually under the table so she couldn't see what he was doing. "By the way, GreyC is a mooch, and I know it. It's all right to give her a few bites, but nothing with garlic or onions because they're toxic to cats."

He didn't bother to look guilty he nodded and grinned. "I am a doctor, Mackie, I also have experience with research involving animals. I'd never give GreyC anything to harm her. I figured that after the last time she saw me, and she hissed at me when I tried to help you back at the bunker, I should kiss furry ass by sharing my burger."

His statement made her smile, and she couldn't help the tingling running rampant through out her body, this man would be so easy to love. Remembering the sight of his naked body made her aware of the fact she was already in lust with him, well that memory, and the trickle of liquid she felt soaking her panties.

The one thing that still bothered her needed to be hashed out before she went to bed tonight. "While you're in a good mood, how about telling me what set you off in such a pissy mood at the store, I'm not criticizing, I want to understand. One minute you were smiling and seemed happy, the next you turned into Mr. Ice." She stood, went to the fridge and grabbed a couple more beers, if the look on his face was anything to go by, this could be a long story.

She had serious doubts that he was going to tell her anything, his face was back to that stoic appearance, and his eyes were narrowed as he looked away from her. So she busied herself by cleaning up the kitchen and putting away the leftovers. They'd used paper plates, so that was easily taken care of, and all she had to wash was the frying pan. Once that was done and she wiped down the counter, she didn't bother to sit down, just took her beer and wandered into the living room. She sat on the couch and picked up the TV remote. The ten o'clock news was on so she left the volume low, and laid back on the leather cushions behind her. He didn't owe her a thing, even a simple explanation.

He joined her during the weather forecast, and she didn't say a word as he sat on the floor near her leg that was propped up on the low table in front of her. When his head dropped on her thigh, she placed her hand on the side of his head and absently rubbed her fingers through his hair. She allowed her fingers to explore his ear and down to his jaw, slowly trailing back to the thick softness of his hair. Once the news was done, she shut the TV off and sat there with him, waiting for him to make the next move. It didn't take long before he began talking, and she didn't interrupt.

"The answer isn't simple, nothing about my life has been simple." He rubbed his cheek against her thigh, and stretched his legs out. "I know it's hard to believe, but I was a runt when I was born. I stayed small until I turned ten or so, and although I kept growing taller, no matter how much or what I ate, I stayed skinny, I'm not talking slender, I'm talking walking skeleton. I tried to eat everything fattening that I could find, and for a skinny kid in a family of grossly overweight people, my life was a living hell. I was tall, but I had no strength, and the family accused me of everything from anorexic to being adopted or switched at birth."

He sat up and pulled one of her legs over his head as he ducked down to scoot over the few inches needed for him to sit between her legs. When he was comfortable, he laid his head back on the cushion between her thighs and reached for her hand to place on top of his head.

Mackie had to smile at his action, but she dutifully began playing with his hair and she would have sworn she heard him purr when she pulled at the strands in her fingers. The second time she pulled, she was certain of it. He started talking again, and she continued caressing him.

"My parents are southern, and a man never lets a woman open her own door, step from a car into a mud puddle, or, and especially, lift heavy objects. My dad was old school and if his sons didn't treat a woman in what he called a decent way there was hell to pay. I could easily take care of the doors and the mud puddles, but the lifting was ridiculously hard for me to do. You can have no idea of the whippings I got for allowing my mother to lift a bucket of mash to feed the chickens, or the way I had to roll bales of hay to feed the farm animals instead of bucking a bale and tossing it in the feeding bin. They all laughed when I got good grades in school. My mother used to say that "book learnin' ain't gonna get you a good job". My dad just got tired of beating on me and called me a faggot and a pussy boy, amongst other flattering names. I left home the day after high school graduation, and never went back. Three days of being homeless on the streets had me signing up for the Army."

He turned his head and kissed the inside of her thigh, and she felt the caress through the material of her slacks, and gave his hair a good pull. He groaned and kissed the spot again. His hands slipped between the material of her pants and her ankles, and slid up to the knee, then he began to lightly massage her muscles.

"I learned a lot in the service, in fact my drill sergeant made it his business to feed me up and muscle me out. I started medical school because I was uniquely qualified for it, according to the tests they kept giving me. I still never figured out what made them continue to hand me test after test, and I aced almost all of them. They figure my IQ is somewhere in the idiot range. According to most of the people

I've talked to, I should be sitting in a corner with chalk and an infinite slate board, drooling and shitting myself while I concentrated on the problem I was working on.

"Instead I am what you see, a man with the ability to cypher crazy things, remember anything I've ever read, and have flaws. I need to be needed in my personal relationships, and I have sexual masochistic streak a mile wide."

He pulled up his legs and rolled his body without breaking from the center of her legs. He went to his knees in front of her and pulled her hands into his, bringing each one up in turn to kiss her palm. "I'm asking you to humor me here. The next time there's something heavy to lift, even something as simple as a bucket, or a thirty pound box of cat litter, allow me to deal with it. Some things a man never gets rid of, and I feel like that weak kid whose own father couldn't stand the sight of when that happens. I know you're capable, and I admire that, but it takes me back, and I try not to go on that trip as much as possible."

Mackie didn't know what to say, the lonely little boy was begging for understanding and she knew that she would do her best to make sure he never felt less than the man he was around her. The sexual masochistic comment touched a chord deep inside of her and if he was indeed a submissive in the bedroom, the idea made her nipples harden and the liquid almost gushed from her pussy.

"So let me get this right, if I told you that I want you to wash my back in the shower, you would do it? Or, if after the shower, I wanted something more from you, you would feel happy to do what I wanted you to do?"

He smiled and nodded his head. "Anything you want me to do, yes. I would love to be your bed slave when you're in the mood to order someone around. I won't spank you if that's what you like, but Liam will, he's a bossy sucker and likes to control everyone. I'm not into pain, but a soft flogging sometimes brings my nerve endings to attention. I might even trust you to flog my back and ass while I'm licking your pretty little pussy. I won't lie and tell you I will allow it right away, but the idea excites me. Right now I'd love to step into the shower with you and wash your back, and anything else you allow me to touch."

He leaned onto her chest and found her parted lips with his. His hands were busy with the buttons on her blouse, and she felt his calloused fingers skim the skin exposed over the top of her bra. She whimpered when his mouth left hers to trail kisses down her jaw and neck.

His words made her hands grab handfuls of his hair as he told her what he wanted to do with her, if that was what she wanted him to do.

"I want to bath you, and shave your pussy lips, so I can lick you until you open your legs for me to taste the sweet salty cream from your pussy. I want to feel you tremble in my arms while I lick and suck every drop from your body and coax more to fill my thirst. I want to know where to touch you to give you the most pleasure a man can give a woman, and then I want to slide my cock as deep inside of you as I can get and rock us into a white hot orgasm."

His hands pulled her breasts from their cotton covering, and mere seconds later his mouth latched onto her nipple, pulling the other nipple between his fingers and rolling it while he sucked on its twin. He switched breasts, giving each equal treatment, and she only became aware that her legs were wrapped around his waist and she was pulling him closer with the muscles in her thighs and calves, when the left one cramped. Her hands had left his hair and were grasping his shoulders with her fingers digging into the soft t-shirt he wore.

Trying to move the leg into a more comfortable position didn't work, and John drew back when he heard her whimper of pain. He looked confused, but her "cramp" brought his attention to her leg.

"Oh you poor thing, I hate when that happens, hang on, sugar, let me help you with that."

His hands gently pushed into the muscle where it had knotted and initially there was a sharper pain, but the muscle began to relax, and she sighed in relief. Her hand ran over his hair and she grabbed a handful of the thickness and pulled his head up to look at her face. "Thank you, and thank you for the pleasure. I guess it's a good thing I got that cramp, I need a shower before I indulge in anything heavier than we've done. So, does that offer to be my body slave still hold? I think I need some help with washing my back, if the offer is still good."

His answering grin and at the quickness he stood made her smile. She glanced down and swallowed, her hand reached out to touch, but he shook his head and took her hand to lead her to the shower.

In the big bathroom he undressed her slowly, so slowly she would begin to think of her scars, and he would kiss each one that was revealed to his eyes. He licked the thin whip marks running from her spine to the back of her neck, and by the time he led her into the shower, she was ready to melt into a puddle without the water that streamed over her breasts and he soaped with his bare hands that made her feel so soft and desirable. She was standing with her back toward him, and her hands were planted on the tiled wall for balance as her back was soaped and massaged. She squeaked when soapy hands slid down the length and into the slit of her ass and pussy.

When he began talking, she fell deeper into bliss.

"I love the feel of your body, tell me, sugar, does it feel good when I play with your clit like this?" Her "uhm", made him grin, and he slid his fingers up into her tight slit and groaned himself. "I want to find every spot that brings you pleasure, but right now, I think I'm getting as much pleasure as you are, I can feel how tight your little pussy is around my fingers, and imagining my cock being squeezed inside of you makes me harder still." His fingers fucked her for as long as it took her to start pushing back faster and harder than he was fucking her. He pulled his fingers from her grasping hole and kissed his way along her shoulders. A dab more liquid soap on his fingers and he ran them up and down between the cheeks of her ass, stopping to gently push one finger inside to the first knuckle.

"Tell me what you feel, I don't want to hurt you, but if this will give you pleasure I'm happy to teach you about the fantastic orgasms you can have from anal fucking." He sent the finger to the second knuckle and felt her begin to shiver. He couldn't believe how responsive her body was, and he leaned harder on her back to get her to bend more. "That's it, baby, you are so beautiful, I'm going to use another finger now, and it might be strange for a few minutes, but you will get used to it, and if you decide to stop me, I will quit. Are you ready?" He saw her back raise and knew that she had taken a deep breath to gear up for something that might or might not be enjoyable. His smile stayed in place as he slowly added another finger, stretching her sphincter wide enough to allow both of his fingers to penetrate the tight opening.

Mackie braced as best she could, expecting pain, but the pain never came. There was a slight burn, but nothing that would cause her to put a stop to what he was doing. Then he added the second finger, the feeling was so strange she let out the breath that she had been holding. The burning continued, and she had a moment of doubt until his fingers began to move while they were inside of her untried asshole. "That feels so weird, and it burns, but I don't see the big deal. Oh, I," the feeling that his wiggling fingers caused deep inside of her ass began to feel unbelievably good. The stretching was still there, as was the fullness, this was different, it gave her, "Oh fuck, that feels good." She pushed back on his fingers and he ran his fingers across the top of her ass, back and forth as she moved on his hand.

"I told you that it would feel good, sugar, just let it take you, I'm right here, I'll catch you. Lord but you're beautiful, I can feel your ass clenching on my fingers, the heat of your body is unbelievable." He moved his free hand down and around the front of her body until he reached her clit. "Here you go, baby, this will help you."

His fingers rubbed her clit hard, and she wouldn't have stopped the orgasm tearing through her body even if she could have. Her body jerked and spasmed, her pussy clamped down on nothing and she felt the wetness slide down onto her thigh. The fingers in her rear end stayed in place until the last jerk of her hips. She stayed where she was for long minutes, allowing the heated water to slide down her back and falling from the sensitive lips of her pussy and stinging asshole.

She reached back to touch him, but he was no longer there. He was standing outside of the shower, holding a towel with a smile on his face. She turned around and made sure all of the soap was rinsed off before she shut the water off and stepped into his arms.

He dried her as tenderly as he could when she laid her body against his. "Come on, sugar, let's find you a place to lay down, and I'll see if I can perk you up and tire you out so you can sleep like a baby."

They walked down the hall and into her bedroom. He led her to the bed, but she had other ideas. She might be tired, but he had a beautiful hard cock she wanted to explore and the idea of ordering him around a bit made her happy.

"I want you to lay down right in the middle of the bed." He gave her a brilliant smile and she knew he was going to enjoy what she planned as much as she would. Put your hands up over your head and keep them there until I say you can lower them." He complied, looking like a sexy buffet and she climbed onto the bed to kneel next to his hip. She set her fingers exploring, while she bent to kiss his smiling lips. They were both breathing heavily when she broke the kiss and continued to explore his athletic body, "You call me beautiful, but I see you like this and it makes me go all squishy inside. I want to explore every inch of you with my hands, my lips…" She followed her fingers with her kisses and licks until she was at his hip, and without warning she licked the trickle of pre-cum from the head of his cock.

He let out a strangled groan, so she did it again. She took the head of his cock between her lips and sucked hard, drawing the thick length deeper into her mouth. One of her hands fondled his sac and the other reached up on his chest to rub and lightly pinch his hard nipples. Hearing his moans and gasps gave her even more incentive to give him as much pleasure as she could wring from him, and she began sliding her head up and down keeping as much suction on his cock as she could. She pinched the wrinkled sac of his balls and felt them draw up tighter. His hips tried to move, but she let go of his sac and pushed his hip down. She wouldn't draw this out too long, but the pleasure he received would be all from her doing.

He called out that he was going to come, and she nibbled on the skin just below the dark pink head of his cock as she felt the pulses coursing through the satin covered hardness. She took him into the back of her throat and hummed with satisfaction as she felt the liquid offering shooting from his cock. She swallowed as fast as she could, and continued to hold him inside the heat of her mouth as his cock began to soften. Each time she gave the retreating flesh a suck, he jerked and shivered, but never asked her to stop. She reluctantly let him go and left her head on his lower belly for a few seconds before sitting up, and placing a kiss on his mouth. "Thank you."

He made her giggle when he asked, "Can I bring my arms down now, Mistress?"

At her nod, his arms came down around her and tossed her over his body to lay next to his side. He spent several minutes kissing her, "I can taste myself in your kiss, do you know how sexy that is? You told me thank you, but it should be me thanking you. That was incredible. I love the smile you're wearing, sugar, I think seeing you wearing nothing but a smile will be my favorite look on you.

"I need to go down and lock things up, why don't you slide under the covers and I'll be right back. Do you need a glass of water or anything?" She nodded, and he leaned down for one more kiss before climbing off the bed and leaving the room.

When he got back, she was asleep, and he climbed in beside her, spooning her backside and wondering if she would stay with them. She felt so good in his arms, and her smile made him smile in return. He closed his eyes and drifted to sleep with her smile pictured in his mind.

Chapter 13

Liam was pulling his hair again, and Darryl laughed softly. "Look, buddy, we half suspected that this was part of the problem all along. The attacks were just too random for them to be connected, and we knew it." He reached over to the man in the passenger seat and squeezed his shoulder. "Look at it this way, half of our problem has been contained."

He nodded but it still pissed him off, they'd caught Hitchcock and his buddy before the two thieving bastards could figure out a way to remove Drummond from the offices. If he hadn't walked in the room when he did, they might have killed his father. Drummond had not exactly been shy about verbally busting the two men that tried to blackmail and cheat his family out of their company. In fact, the officers that came in answer to the 911 call Darryl had placed were forced to physically restrain Drummond when Hitchcock began rattling off his threats to the Klinger family.

Liam rested his head on the headrest. "What bugs me is how Hitchcock knew about us. I think we need to do a security sweep in every residence and office that we're known to frequent. How much classified information has already been leaked?"

He didn't want to tell Darryl about the innuendos the man had made against Darryl.

He'd been talking about the big bad bastard getting his too, but that it wasn't his issue. If Hitchcock knew about another threat, this time against Darryl, what could he do to find out what the threat was, and from who? He would wait until they got to the house, and maybe John would be up so they could all discuss the problem at one time.

Darryl pulled into the drive-thru and ordered burgers for their dinner. Once they'd dropped Drummond off, they took his Mercedes to go home in. The girl behind the window checked out the car and complimented him on his wheels, and batted her heavily mascara laden lashes at him, which made Darryl smile and shake his head. He wasn't into teeny boppers, she giggled at him when he smiled at her as she handed him his change. *Little girl was going to get herself in trouble one of these days with that shit.*

Liam laughed as they pulled away. "You know, back in the day either one of us would've been getting her number and trying to impress her with our moves." He finished the French fry he was chewing on, "Damn I feel old sometimes."

"The real fucked up thing about that is that both of us are old enough to be her father. Can you imagine having a girl that age and knowing most of the male species would be chasing after her like we used to do? I would have a coronary, or be in jail. Damned if I wouldn't."

Darryl almost choked on his burger, "Goddammit, what did you have to say something like that for? I've been picturing our girl with a big belly, and you had to bring that up. Up till now I thought it would be nice to have a little girl hellion to spoil and teach how to defend herself from bastards like us. Now that I remember how I was, fuck, no girls allowed. Mackie is enough female for any household.

"We had a good time today before we came into town. If we hadn't run out of time, I'd planned to take her down to the lake and do something romantic. I got the feeling she hasn't been romanced much, or if she has, it wasn't something she felt was romantic. She looks good covered in dirt and mud." He grinned as Liam laughed.

"I was semi hard the whole time we played today, she had me so wound up that I came close to begging her to let me lick her pussy right in the field." He was busy watching traffic and eating his burger, but thinking about the way she smiled, and what he wanted to do with those lips.

Liam finished the last bite and washed it down with his favorite strawberry flavored shake. "Let's hope she decides to stay. I've been fascinated by her since the day she threatened to kill me for hurting Eric. I'd been dreaming of her face since that night in the bunker, and let me tell you, I woke up harder than the normal morning wood. I didn't make it

to the shower to jack off a couple of times."
Recalling waking up soaked in his own semen
didn't embarrass him, it happened to most men
at times.

"I turned Gloria Waxford down because
she's a petite blonde, I wanted a bigger girl
with big breasts and an ass that I could grab
onto without worrying I'd break her fucking her.
I wanted a woman with light brown hair and
blue eyes that isn't afraid to look a man in the
eyes when she talks to him."

Darryl was nodding his head in agreement.
"You should be standing next to her for a few
hours and then tell me about what you want in
a woman. I'd lay good money on the fact you
wouldn't be thinking about another woman. I
keep thinking that we can't let this one walk
away, Liam. You and John might not be
convinced that she's the love we've been
dreaming and talking about for so long, but I
am. I love you guys, you both know that, but I
won't give her up without a fight."

He stayed silent for the next few minutes to
let Liam digest his declaration of intent. Then
he explained what happened earlier at the
office building, changing the subject without
changing the people they'd been discussing,
and told him about Mackie's involvement.

"When we figured out that you were
sending us a message, she was already
peeling off the suit jacket and fluffing her hair. It
was like she'd been reading my mind before I
opened my damn mouth. There's no fear in her

when it's time for doing. I can maybe count on one hand the number of women I've met with the kind of courage she has."

Liam agreed with him, seeing her stride into the room, ignoring the man with the gun, she'd gone straight for the easier target, and kicked his ass. "Let me tell you something to really give you a stiffy. She's not just good with weapons and explosives, she had Hitchcock swallowing his balls within seconds of walking in the door."

They continued to talk about the fight, until they pulled into the driveway and parked in front of the barn. On the walk to the house, Liam confessed, "About Mackie, you're not alone in feeling more than like for her. I've been in love and lust with her in that order since laying eyes on the woman, and it makes no sense, but it's there and nothing has changed since then. My dad said the same thing happened when he met Mom, he wanted to pick her up and find a cave somewhere."

The house was dark except for the kitchen light, and they tried to be as quiet as possible when they walked into the house. It wasn't quite midnight but Darryl locked the door and headed upstairs with Liam two steps behind him. He slowly opened Mackie's bedroom door and smiled when he saw the two figures spooning under the covers. The small amount of light from the hallway's nightlights cast a shadow of his form near the bed, and he backed away, but waved Liam over to take a peek at the slumbering couple.

He envied John his place on that mattress tucked into the curve of Mackie's back and thighs. If he weren't so tired, he might have joined them. Knowing he would wake them if he did made him back away from the door and close it softly before heading to his room.

Mackie didn't know what to expect when she went down the stairs to the kitchen the next morning. John had been gone for a while because his pillow was cold when she touched it, but she'd lain there for an extra ten minutes remembering the strange relationship that was developing between her and the three men that claimed to want to share her amongst them. It didn't seem fair to her that one woman could possibly hold the attention and devotion of three wonderful guys, when so many women were desperately looking for just one man to hold her at night. In the past, she'd always fallen back on her self image and background to avoid entanglements with men she considered out of her league. These men had proven that her visible scars weren't a deterrent, or ugly. Now she needed to battle her inner demons if she really believed they could build a relationship and life together.

She couldn't remember a time that she hadn't been lonely. Way back in the beginning when she'd escaped the drug house with all of the dead bodies lying in pools of blood, she'd gotten her freedom, but no one to take care of or be taken care of was left, she was on her own. Louisa had been a major disappointment, but who could blame her, once she had a home to live in and food to eat. The woman had stolen over half of the money and two of the deeds to properties close by, and left when Mackie graduated from high school. She had never looked back, and Mackie didn't chase after the woman, even if she had cried after she saw Louisa drive away for the last time. The closest thing to a family she'd ever had was Laura and Thom, but they had kids of their own, plus they would be moving away from her too. As soon as Laura retired from public office next year, they'd be gone.

She refused to base her decision about the men on a need for company. She wanted to belong, to have a family of her own, but she wouldn't allow desperation to be part of her reason for being with the men. She thought back to laying in the hospital bed talking to Laura and lying when she said she didn't remember the men. She remembered them all right, and as soon as she'd gotten out of the hospital and settled in her room at the Senator's house, the stalking began.

First, she'd researched Darryl Reynolds. There was nothing in the small pockets of information of what he'd disclosed to her yesterday, only his business dealings and a divorce over a decade ago. After talking to him and hearing his story, it made her wonder if having a family was worth the heartbreak she knew he'd faced at the time.

John Fielding was a wonder boy with several degrees that had been obtained during and after his hitch in the service. He had been photographed with a few stunning women, almost all tall and slender with varying shades of red hair. The pictures she'd seen had made her laugh when looking at his face. The women were hanging onto his arm as if he might escape at any time, and his face showed that he might if he could just get those long fingernails pried out of the sleeve of his suit coat. He had also developed several medical equipment improvements, and as with Darryl's family, there had been no mention of them.

Liam was the center hub of the men, she could see that without having read so many articles that actually said nothing of a personal nature, other than the well known stats of the second son in a family that only had to sneeze to make a million dollars. He was considered a brilliant businessman, but a pitifully poor object for the matrimonial minded females looking for a well heeled spouse.

People who were interviewed joked the three men were joined in a bond so tight that if one were to die, the other two would eat bullets to keep him company in hell. Two women had been interviewed for an expose on the families of the rich and famous, and the women swore they had been in a very heavy sexual relationship with the three men, but they never elaborated on the break-up. Or even why they no longer enjoyed being a "Love Slave" to the kinky trio.

Individual women who had dated the men one on one smiled and said very little when asked about each man. All in all her research had been disappointing to say the least. No one knew about the elaborate security set up, the vital research, or even Dorian. If she'd still been in the FBI, she would have been able to access more in depth information, but from what she was seeing, there would be very little to discover.

The kitchen was empty, but the new pot of coffee was waiting for her to help herself and she wasted no time pouring a cup. There was a box of toaster waffles on the counter, and she looked to see if the box was empty. There was two left in the plastic package, and a small plastic pillow pack of syrup sat next to the box, so she popped the things down in the toaster and she grabbed a small plate and fork to eat her breakfast with.

The men came in from outside while she was washing her plate and setting it in the drainer. They brought in the crisp scent of sunshine and fresh air, and she smiled. "I wondered what happened to you guys. Thank you for the coffee by the way. I finished off the waffles, so you might need to put them on the shopping list." She was standing in front of the sink, and the three men stood less than five feet from her, smiling at her without saying anything to break the awkwardness that she was feeling. "What? Look, I'm not familiar with morning after rituals, the few men I've been with have been gone within an hour after sex, so I need some kind of direction here."

Liam stepped right up to her and bent his head to kiss her on the lips, but she turned her head and his lips landed next to her ear. "You can't say good morning, or hello or," his lips captured hers and his tongue sliding between her teeth silenced her for the length of time it took to steal her breath and his hands to roam over her hips and the cheeks of her ass.

He drew his head back and looked at her face with that drowsy look that his kiss had put there, and he smiled. "Good morning, beautiful. We walked in and saw you standing there with the sun behind you, and you have to forgive me, but you looked so delicious that it took me a minute to decide which part of the picture to start kissing. I'm just a man, sugar, the sight of you makes me stupid with hunger for you. The blood leaves my brain and goes straight south."

The sound of chairs being pulled out from the table and someone pouring coffee intruded on the small moment, but she could feel the evidence of his words lying hard between his body and hers. He was hard, and she melted. "Like I said, I'm not familiar with how things work around here yet."

He stepped back, held one hand out, and escorted her the four steps it took for her to reclaim the chair she'd sat in earlier. Her coffee had been refreshed and each man had a cup in front of him too.

Liam looked at each of them in turn, and began talking. "We have reason to believe the threat isn't over with yet. Yesterday Hitchcock was spouting off at the mouth, and I saw him looking at Darryl across the room, and he was mumbling about how he was going to get his soon enough. Someone else is after Darryl, someone who apparently got the information from Hitchcock on Darryl's whereabouts and tried to get to him at the Pub."

Mackie looked toward the big man and waited for him to put a name to the suspected people that would wish him harm. He said nothing. In fact he appeared to be skeptical when Liam disclosed the possible threat.

John was watching Darryl too, and he was frowning. "Okay, man, spill. We can see that you suspect someone, or you'd be hitting the computer to look at the list you keep of possible threats and disgruntled ex-employees."

GreyC decided to join the people. Apparently it was time they became used to being her slaves, since she traveled from lap to lap under the table top, and popped her head up from Liam's arm, put both paws onto the table, and hopped the rest of the way onto the shiny wooden surface. She went to Darryl and sat in front of him curling her tail around her haunches.

It was too much of a coincidence for John and he burst out laughing. "See? Even the cat knows you're holding out on us."

Darryl patted his chest, and GreyC rose on her back legs to place her front paws on the place he'd used to signal her. She licked his nose and batted at his mouth, and he let her head butt him before he gathered her into his arms and began rubbing her belly. He looked up and began talking.

"The siblings are fighting with the old man over money as usual, and he tried to pull at my heart strings by reminding me that they are his kids too, and I should treat them better. They want new cars and he says he doesn't have the money, but thinks that since I work for you, I should pony up and buy them cars. I said something like I'll buy those two snot faced brats cars when I'm dead in the ground, because that's the only way they'd get a penny from me." He scratched the furball's ears, and continued, "I guess he wasn't joking when he said that could be arranged. I knew that he didn't give a shit about me and my mom, but when he said that, I told him to bring it. Maybe he accepted the challenge."

He looked at Liam and asked, "What am I worth dead? Maybe a few million? If they succeed in killing me off, they'll think it's Christmas, at least until the will is read. My mother's estate is supposed to go to any children that I may have, if not, it goes to the family on her side. I made it that way so blood family would get it before him and his little leeches did. Letting them have what was my mother's would be like slapping her in the face, and he caused her enough grief when she lived. So I guess dear old Dad is going the more direct route to the money, and he doesn't know about the patents. He thinks he'll get Mom's money if I die." GreyC bit his thumb when he quit petting her for a second and he frowned at the demanding feline.

She sniffed at him, walked out of his arms, and over to John for him to pay her, her dues. Everyone smiled at the cat's actions, and Mackie felt like they'd passed some sort of test in her mind. GreyC knew better than to plop her butt on the table, but these new people were allowing her to get away with it, and she was taking advantage of the fact. "You know that she's going to be hard to break from hopping on the table from now on, right? I almost had her broken of the habit back at my house, and at the Senator's place, she wasn't allowed in the kitchen or dining rooms. Now she's testing her limits, and you're falling for a furry face and naughty girl attitude."

John looked at the cat and the cat looked at him, reached up a paw and patted him on the cheek. He gathered her into his arms and buried his face in her fur. Liam shook his head and grinned at Mackie.

"Your cat spent most of the night sleeping on my chest. This morning, she got pissed off because I didn't get up early enough for her satisfaction, so she sank her claws into my chest to wake me up. When I sat up, she went flying to the foot of the bed, so she has been nice to me this morning, once she did her thing, and ate a slice of ham. She doesn't seem to like that crunchy dry stuff you have in the dish."

Mackie couldn't believe what she was hearing and seeing from these men. "Have any of you ever had a pet before?" Three heads shook back and forth, and Darryl shrugged his shoulder.

"We had horses, but they were mostly show animals and my mother loved them." He looked at his folded hands and seemed to be lost in memories.

Mackie grinned, no wonder they didn't realize GreyC was playing them, GreyC was the first pet they'd ever had around. She should put a stop to spoiling the cat, but she decided to let them find out for themselves, just like she had to do when dealing with them.

Darryl got up and rinsed his cup, and addressed the room in general. "I think I'll see if telling the old man that he gets nothing, and his snot nosed brats get nothing when I die, changes his plans. In fact, maybe I'll tell him I'm leaving everything to the overseas relatives that hate his guts almost as much as I do. He can argue familial status then, but those people could buy and sell all of us and it wouldn't put a dent in the checkbook."

Chapter 14

John left shortly after the coffee klatch broke up, and since Darryl had left the room to deal with his father, that left her and Liam sitting at the table. Liam put the furball on the floor and looked at her with a smile.

"I have the day off, so what would you like to do? I can imagine how strange this setup is, so maybe you just want to veg for the day and hang out. Or we can take the four-wheelers down to the trails and commune with nature. It's too cold to skinny dip in the lake, but it's a beautiful spot, very peaceful and private." He stood to put his cup in the sink, and added, "I'm dying to know all about you, because you are a woman with secrets, and I like secrets, as long as I'm in on them. I have to make a call, but why don't we meet back here in half an hour and you can tell me what we're doing today?"

He gave her a smile, but it was the determined look in his eyes when he'd mentioned her secrets that bothered her. The man was no dummy. He'd probably ordered a full report on her the minute he'd remembered her name. She knew exactly what the records showed, and it was entirely statistics. High school and up into the past few years hiring out as security. She had a good reputation for doing her job, but personal matters were noticeably absent. Not that she had a private life to worry about, still, if she had one, she would do her damndest to keep it private. *Screw it, you don't have to tell him a damn thing. It's not like you had a choice back then, and now you have the choice to tell or not tell about Texas.*

She washed the coffee carafe and put the cups in the dishwasher before deciding to explore the house a bit more. Maybe she would decide what she wanted to do for the day while she was snooping. She was used to men, but not in a situation like this was. Why did life have to be so complicated anyway?

Darryl was ready to pinch the old man's head off at the neck, and he didn't bother to involve the other men in this, it was time to demonstrate that he would back up his words. The man actually called him a few names and threatened his "fuck buddies" if he didn't pony up some cash. By "some cash" he'd rattled off his needed amount of, "Two hundred thousand dollars, and you and your fuck buddies can carry on with whatever it is you do."

Enough was enough, he would stop this today, and the old man could go straight to hell. He thought about texting Liam, but decided the man deserved to have Mackie to himself for a few hours, and his mission with the old fucker wouldn't take much time. The Harley started and he felt the satisfaction of knowing the powerful bike was intimidating to his father. The man had always been deathly afraid of motorcycles after his best friend had been killed by a woman who'd been drinking and driving while he was driving past the side street that she pulled out from without seeing the biker. Darryl had been forbidden to purchase a bike until he was old enough to go on his own to buy one. This bike was purchased the summer his mother had died, and he kept it in perfect shape.

He pulled the bike into the circular driveway and was disappointed to see four vehicles in the parking area, but he wasn't going to leave, no, this would be finished today. The front door was ajar and opened when he put his knuckles to the wood. He stepped inside of the door and waited for some sign that people were there.

A muffled sound from directly across the entrance hall gave him a direction to go and he slowly walked along the dirty area rug lining the wide passage. The voices from the other side of the door sounded angry, and he didn't resist snooping by turning the door handle slowly and pushing it open just enough to see what was going on. He had expected the old guy to be fucking one of his pickups, but what he saw pissed him off.

Two men stood over his father, who was sitting in a chair tied to the legs and arms of the thing with silver Duct tape. He could see his father's face, and even with the swollen face and bloody nose, he felt no pity for the man who should have been his best friend. He pushed the door just a little wider and saw Chrissy and another man, who must be her newest patsy, sitting on the couch, scowling at a barely awake DE, telling him to think of a way to get the money, or die.

He pulled the door back, almost shut, and turned to leave. Fuck it, the bastard was getting what he'd deserved, it was a shame he wasn't the one to draw blood on the arrogant bastard, but he would be out of everyone's misery by the time those men were finished.

He was seated on the bike when he felt a sense of, hell, it was a creepy feeling running on his spine. He would deny hearing his mother telling him to do the right thing, but he heard her soft voice asking him to do the right thing, "*For me.*" He looked around hoping to see another source the voice could be coming from, but no one was there, and he hung his head. He whispered in answer, "For you," and stood away from the bike.

Luckily the seat slid back to show a small compartment that held a 1911, and a sheathed knife. He held the blade considering what his best options for saving the man he hated more than anything or anyone on the face of the earth.

His booted foot kicking the solid wood back on its hinges and the way he rolled into the room shooting his father's assailants in the leg and gut respectively caused surprised screams from Chrissy, and the man next to her never knew what happened. Darryl ended up behind Chrissy and her man, holding his gun to the fucker's neck. She was screaming bloody murder, and he laughed at her when the boyfriend grabbed her arm when she started to get up to run.

"Well, well, what do we have here? You boys should have had better taste than to hook up with her, but I saw her naked once, so I can see where you'd let a easy piece of ass lead you around by the dick, problem is, you'll find out she isn't worth the trouble you're in now." He tapped the muzzle on the guy's temple. "You need to tell your boys to take a breath and not do anything stupid, you're not a friend of mine, and your death won't mean a thing to Chrissy here. A cunt like her deserves to be behind bars, don't you think? While you boys are serving time, you can take comfort knowing that she's learning to watch her ass in the women's lock-up."

They could hear sirens outside, and one of the men on the floor picked up the gun he'd dropped when he grabbed his thigh from Darryl's shot. "I ain't going back." The dumbass held the gun to his own head and pulled the trigger, but the angle he held it and the recoil sent the barrel up away from the killing zone and barely grazed his skull.

Darryl shook his head, "Real competent men you have there, slick, tell me, did you pick them out, or are they men Chrissy found to help? Did you ask them if she was a good fuck before you tossed your fate in with them?"

The man that he'd shot in the gut was moaning, and Darryl knew he was in pain, but that little devil inside of him was dancing with happiness to know he was the cause of that painful gasp and cry.

The police came rushing through the door with guns drawn and ordered Darryl to put the gun down and lie flat on the floor. He assumed the position, and waited for the cop to check his license and concealed carry permits. After that, he helped them piece things together, and saw his father loaded into the ambulance, before locking the place up for the night after the police had finished doing their thing, and the place emptied out.

He had another stop before he could go home, and hoped that his involvement in the whole thing was over with, but Karma is a bitch, and once he saw his half siblings, he knew he was sunk.

The boy answered the door and tried to slam it shut before Darryl could introduce himself. The size fourteen boot kept the door from shutting, and the kid still tried to hold the door closed. Darryl was out of sorts, and he put his voice of doom, as John called it, into telling the kid to knockoff the bullshit.

"You obviously know who I am, and I don't have the interest or tolerance for this shit. Open the fucking door or I'll do it for you."

The kid denied knowing him, so Darryl pulled his cell phone out of its case and pretended to call his new friends at the cop shop.

"Hey, Officer Samson, I'm here at the house where the kids are, yeah, they won't open the door to me or even talk, so I guess you'll need to send social services out here as soon as possible." He decided to goad the skinny kid and when Samson asked the kids' ages, he turned his head and said, "I'm not exactly sure, the boy might be twelve, maybe thirteen, he's acting pretty scared, and the girl is nowhere to be seen. She's probably hiding in a closet or something. I'll wait outside for you to get here, yeah, okay see you."

Hearing the, "Sixteen, you asshole, I'm sixteen, and Ginny is fourteen, and I'm not afraid of you," the kid yelled from the other side of the door made him shrug, and put the phone back into its case.

Darryl sat down on the step, and waited the boy out. He hadn't called Samson, he dialed his own number and left the message. If the threat of social services didn't rattle the brat's cage enough to open the door and talk to him, then he really would make the call. A girl came around the side of the house and headed right for him, and from the looks of her, he'd have to guess that this was Ginny.

She was slender to the point of painfully thin, and her hair hung down to her elbows. What grabbed his attention were her eyes. He knew those eyes, he looked at them every morning in the mirror. Their paternal grandfather had the same green eyes, and even though he could see nothing else to show that she was related to him, they were proof enough.

Her opening salvo made it official. "It's about time you showed up. You know, for a brother you really suck. We used to see pictures of you at our dad's, and he would make us put them away so Chrissy wouldn't see them and raise hell." She came closer and sat next to him on the step.

Her next words shouldn't have surprised him, but they did, and he looked at her with a small grin.

"So, since you're here, and they're not, I'm guessing the whole killing you for the wads of money didn't work out like they planned." She called over her shoulder for Eddy to come out and join them. "Come on, she can't kill us for letting him in, he's outside, and she didn't say we couldn't go outside, did she?"

She turned back to address him, and Darryl felt that frozen block in his heart melt a little more. She was a scrapper, and he liked her, and decided to get to know her and Eddy better, one way or the other. From the looks of this girl's clothing, and lack of the normal teenaged girl actions, his idea of spoiled brats getting everything handed to them appeared to be mistaken.

"So, what went wrong? Did you lose all of your money in the stock market? Or didn't you have any to begin with? You know Chrissy is going to be disappointed you are here and she isn't, so how about you make it worth our while for all the hell we'll catch when she drags in tonight, or in the morning? You buy pizza, and we'll help you eat it."

He laughed, and handed her his phone. "Make the call, but make sure it's a large with lots of meat and cheese, and I don't eat fungus, so save the mushrooms for you and Eddy."

Eddy opened the door and rattled off the number to the place they knew of, and had enjoyed the pizza from before. Darryl glanced at the boy and knew these kids were far from spoiled. He was wearing a t-shirt that was too tight in the chest and arms. The boy had their father's brown eyes, but he was as skinny as Ginny, possibly more so given that he was a few inches under six feet tall.

He had to tell them, "Your mom's in jail, and your father is in the hospital by now, so I don't think you have to worry about making her mad. He asked me to help you guys out for a few days, so here I am."

Chapter 15

Mackie fed the spoiled furball and made sure the litter box was clean before joining Liam who was wearing jeans and a t-shirt with a long sleeved flannel covering his arms, and she almost laughed. She was wearing the identical outfit, right down to the hiking boots. She told him, "I think we know what we will be doing today, so there won't be any argument from either of us. I'm ready when you are." She walked over to him and nodded. "Yeah, it is spooky, but I seem to be getting used to the connection." She was talking about the way one could look at the other and could almost read the other's mind with some things. The first time she'd laid eyes on him, she felt a connection. It wouldn't have stopped her from shooting him, but it would have saved his life. Again that first night with the men, she'd felt it when he looked at her while he was buried deep inside of John's sexy ass. His look had given her that extra push while Darryl's fingers manipulated her pussy into such an intense orgasm and Liam's expression shoved that orgasm into hyperdrive. She knew his was just as intense at the time. The clothing choice was just another bit of proof to her, he shrugged and smiled before taking her arm and walking to the barn.

They took the quad runners and headed to the lake. The morning air was crisp, but she laughed out loud as they got air flying over several small mounds of heaped dirt and weeds, and she loved it. These men didn't realize the paradise they had here for someone like her. She never had toys as a child, or if she had them before the drug house, she had no memory of it.

The one shrink she'd seen told her that gaps in memory were common when someone had been around drugs in the setting she and the other children had been subjected to. The woman had gotten too friendly and began asking questions about the place she'd been, the names of the people who'd died that night, and even the people she knew who had been killed for drug debts at that time. The frustration the woman displayed when she refused to give her the answers to her questions made the sessions uncomfortable and she felt the woman had ulterior motives, more so than just curiosity. Mackie backed away without continuing therapy after three months.

Two years later, she had been reading missing persons posters in an airport in southern California, and felt guilt when she saw pictures of kidnapped and missing children. Some of the missing had been taken twenty years before the day's date. Once she had gotten back to her rented cabin in Virginia, she'd begun writing a memory journal. The people were named, even the children for what little she had memory of, considering their backgrounds and the stories they told her and the other children about their lives. She included her own birth name and information, but didn't give a clue that she was the one who was writing the journal.

She'd named names of the drug dealers and several standouts in her memory that had run afoul of the evil Jorge and Renaldo. Every extra snippet of information that she knew about was written in the journal. It took her two years to remember everything, and then find the time to put her memories into a word document. She omitted the part about her taking the money and deeds to various properties, they didn't need to know anything about her life after the fact.

When it was finished, she read it in its entirety, and wondered how such evil could exist in the world. It took her another six months of feeling guilt for withholding information from families of the children who were like the ones begging for information about the whereabouts of their loved ones. She made three copies of the disk and sent one to the FBI in D.C. and one to the Attorney General of Texas.

She still had her copy and the hard drive from the computer she'd used to write the journal on in a bank vault in Ann Arbor, Michigan. Her spirit lifted slowly, but sending the information off to people who might be able to connect the dots correctly gave her such a feeling of relief that she knew she'd done the correct thing.

She wondered what a shrink would say about the relationships she was considering going into with open eyes, and a needy heart. She guarded her emotional side for so long that she didn't trust her own judgment in relationships with men. Now, she had the opportunity to have three men that accepted her as she was and even appeared to love her differences from what she considered normal women. Maybe in time she would be able to see her life as normal, yet somehow she doubted it would be anytime soon.

Soon they came through a trail lined with thick trees and waist high undergrowth with hidden roots and small game scurrying out of the path they traveled on with the noisy machines. Liam slowed his quad, and she followed his lead until they stopped at the top of a steep hill leading down to the lake. She thought he meant to hike down, and the idea wasn't thrilling to her. What if she got down there and couldn't climb back up?

Liam lifted the seat of his quad and took out a small folded silver square of material, and walked several feet to their left where an old maple tree was beginning to show off her fall colors in yellows and varying shades of red. He spread the thin blanket on the ground and waved her over to join him.

"This is one of my favorite spots on the property. I come here to find my inner balance a few times a year, and it almost always works to calm me down. Stretch out here and see if you feel the same way as I do." He removed the flannel and pulled his t-shirt over his head and sat down, leaning back on his hands that were propping his torso up. "I love it here, and when Darryl found the place, I would have bought it myself, but all three of us found the beauty of the property irresistible, so we're partners."

Mackie joined him on the silver cloth. "I can see why you guys love the place, I can't imagine wanting to leave very often if you didn't have to." She watched him stretch in the sunlight and enjoyed the view more than she should have, but turned her head toward the lake when her thoughts began to have a more carnal turn. "You have room to breathe and plenty of space to play with whatever toys you can afford to buy. It's great here."

Liam sat up and scooted over to sit behind her with his long legs stretched out on either side of her hips. His hands went to her shoulders and he began to massage the muscles under his fingertips with a firm but gentle touch. She let her head fall back and relaxed her back until he asked her a question she never thought anyone would ask.

"So why don't you tell me about Louisa Vought and her teenaged sister who popped up in Reno fifteen years ago, and how they managed to make it that far with no records or relatives to find."

Her mind went blank, and that old fear from so long ago slid down her spine. The pleasure of the massage forgotten as she tried to remember the backstory Louisa had helped her come up with to deal with nosy intrusive people. "Our parents were killed in a drunk driving accident and we were left on our own, I was home schooled." She shrugged and tried to let the tension fall from her spine, but his hands were still on her shoulders, and she knew he was aware that she lied.

She thought about what she'd just said, and decided to give him at least part of the truth. "Look, she was homeless and I was in a bad situation, so we teamed up and turned ourselves into two respectable sisters with a tragic background and a new life. We weren't wanted by the police, and hadn't done anything wrong or illegal. Can we just leave it at that?"

The hug that she received for her truth made her feel good, for once the past wouldn't ruin her happiness. It wasn't like she lied, and maybe someday she would be able to tell the men about her past, she held no blame for what had happened that night, or any of the other times bad things had happened in the little house before then either. The relief of finally admitting to herself that she had no choice, and that it was a legitimate excuse for staying silent and living as a slave made her want to cry.

Liam contented himself with her bare bones explanation. It was a start, and he hoped she learned to trust him and the others with all of her past, but right now he wanted to thank her and kissing the back of her neck was his favored place to begin. His lips moved across the soft skin to her shoulder and traveled back the way they'd come to the other shoulder. "Thank you for the honesty, sugar, I was hoping you wouldn't lie to me. I want there to be trust between us."

She enjoyed the way his hands reached under her t-shirt and cupped her breasts. She groaned and leaned into his lips as they traveled back to her jawline and nibbled up to her ear. His hands came away from under her shirt to pull the flannel and t-shirt off, and she tried to turn around to face him, but his *shh* stopped her.

"I'm just playing a little for now, sugar, you'll get your turn to torture me soon enough. Why don't you relax, and tell me how you feel about this situation? I know that brain of yours has a million questions, and I'd bet my last dime you wonder how we knew you were the lady we were looking for. You go ahead and ask me anything, I'll just sit here and play with these beauties. I can feel the warmth of the sunshine heating your flesh, can you feel the heat?" His hands released the three deep clasps of her bra, and pulled it completely off her body.

She moaned when his hands shaped the generous globes, and plucked at her tight nipples. "I, ah, how did you guys decide that you were meant to be together?" Her words were whispered but she couldn't concentrate on both questions and sensation. She felt the liquid from her pussy slide from her center and crossed her legs to stop it from completely soaking her pants. She had never been in a position like this, just being teased, and she liked it, her body warmed fast enough to his touch. He was talking and she was trying to listen to him, but it was difficult.

"We met at a fundraiser for Wounded Warriors. It's a non-profit to assist wounded Veterans and their families once the soldier comes home. We've done a fundraiser every year since the project began. Darryl was one of the first men I met when we visited the rehab facility, and he impressed me with his determination and intelligence. John was doing some volunteer work in the same place. Over time we became good friends. John devotes as many hours to the project as he can when he has free time, and Darryl, well that man has more stubbornness in his little finger than most people have in their entire bodies. He and some of his former retired servicemen and women hold poker runs, and toy runs for people in need, the Wounded Warrior Project is another of his passions. He will tell you about his experiences, and there were times I think he wanted to eat a bullet, but something keeps him straight and alive.

"We used to get together and hold meetings for the big party Klinger throws for the fundraisers and those contributors that donated a certain amount of money or time to the cause. John was already working in the lab, and Darryl was finished with rehab from his wounds. He was still in the service but getting ready to leave when his hitch was over, and we all began talking one night. We found out that we had a lot in common, but it still took a good six months before we told each other that we were bi-sexual, and the rest just happened naturally. I would do anything for either of them and I know they love me as much as I do them. Enjoying sex with another man doesn't make any of us less than the men we are, it's just one more layer of pleasure to discover and enjoy."

He pulled her sideways and guided them into lying side by side with him leaning over her, and his lips took each nipple in turn for a gentle kiss and lick. "I love your tits, they're too distracting when I need to talk with you, so I think I should go ahead and do what I've been wanting to do from the first night I saw them." He sucked one into his mouth and pinched and rolled the other between his fingers while molding the rounded flesh with the palms of his hands.

Her hands tangled in his thick hair and she pulled at the strands to get his face as close to her flesh as possible. "Don't stop, that feels so good, please don't stop." The feeling of his mouth sucking and working her nipples with his tongue and fingers sent a direct path to her pussy, and she forgot all about attempting to stem the liquid from escaping and wetting her clothes. His lips moved from one nipple to the other, and she felt the clenching of her inner muscles as her body took over and forced the small scream from between her gritted teeth as she came.

He couldn't resist kissing her again and took her lips roughly, while his hands worked the belt buckle and snap of her jeans. "I can't wait for this, I thought we could make out a little and go home, but I need to taste you, and if you're going to say no, you need to say it now." He pulled her jeans down to her shoes and cursed at the extra minute it took him to untie the laces and pull the boots off, then the denim and scrap of satiny panties she wore was soon on the blanket beside them. He spread her long legs and sat back on his heels to look his fill before bending down and separating the thick lips hiding the object of his thirst. "Oh, sugar, look at this, you're so ready for me, but I want to lick your pussy and make you shake even more when you come on my tongue."

He kissed his way from her clit to just below the entrance of her body and then licked his way back up to her clit. His tongue never ceased to move and as she scored his shoulders with her short fingernails, he moaned. The sound vibrated from him into her clit, and still he continued to lick and suck her from one end to another. He gave her relief of sorts by sliding in a finger as deep as it could go, and finger fucked her for a few minutes before adding a second finger deep into her tunnel. His hand worked side to side and mashed up against the wet pink flesh before sliding away, leaving her lifting her hips seeking to be filled again.

He sat back and got his belt and fly undone before shoving the material down to his knees and scooted closer for his thick cock to kiss the begging invitation of her pussy. "I thought I could wait, but that's not happening, you're just too tempting and I'm too close to coming myself to hold back any longer."

She gasped as his thickness spread her tight hole and he took his time so she could work her hips up to meet his while his fingers pinched her nipples harder than before, and she was crying out from the sensations that filled her body. Her legs encircled his hips and crossed at the ankles surrounding him, securing his hips to her own, even as he gave her everything she needed to achieve the pleasure that waited for both of them on the other side.

"Oh, oh yes, I." That was as coherent as she could be while her breath was singing in and out of her lungs in time with the movements of their hips slamming against one another. Every so often he would rest his cock deep inside of her while he ground his hips down hard over hers, and the way he mashed her clit at those times drove her close to the edge again and again. She held onto his wide shoulders and lifted herself to rain kisses alone his cheeks and collarbone until she felt that deep clenching feeling and the sensations where his body slid over hers became too much to contain. She screamed and tried to hold it back, but her orgasm had begun and nothing would stop it from pulling her away into the floating bright colors in her mind. She jerked in tune with the clench and release of her pussy, and began laughing, urging him on to join her in mutual pleasure. Her hand trailed down his spine and slid down the crease of his ass causing him to double his movements and suddenly slam to a stop, his cock was as deep as it could go as he emptied the cum from his balls with his cock being squeezed inside of her still grasping cunt. He collapsed on her, and she held his face to her breast as they slowly began to breathe normally again.

She hugged him tight to her chest one more time and kissed the top of his head. "Not to be mean here, but if you could take some of your weight off my chest, I might be able to breathe. I love to have you in this position, but it's not the most comfortable."

He lifted his head with a lazy smile and propped his chest up on his arms before bending his head to give each nipple a slow lick and quick kiss. Her legs unhooked at the ankles and fell off to the sides as he sat up and continued to look his fill of the satisfied beauty lying there splayed in such an abandoned way.

"Lady, if you have a hope of getting lunch today, you'll get me motivated to move so you can get dressed, because seeing you like this, after what we just shared, is no motivation to leave here. I could make love to you all day."

Chapter 16

Darryl wasn't sure what to do with two half starved kids like these were, so he told them to pack light for a couple of days, they were going home with him. He wasn't about to stay overnight in their place, and he figured they could use some attention and definitely new clothes. Maybe if he was lucky the guys would be receptive to taking the kids under their wings. He could think of several less than savory people to introduce them to. The situation at the farmhouse might be awkward for everyone, but what could it hurt to keep the kids for the short time his old man was in the hospital. One thing was certain, he wasn't about to give them to their mother without a fight.

He walked outside after sliding the heavy pizza on the table for them to eat their fill. It pissed him off when Eddy waited until his sister grabbed two pieces and the kid stared at him waiting until he pulled a slice off for himself. He could tell the boy was used to waiting for whatever was left and it made him want to strangle his mother. The fridge had a tub of butter substitute, a shelf full of liquor and beer, and a carton of eggs with two left inside of the cardboard. He began opening drawers and cabinet doors to see what the kids normally ate, but the pitiful amount of food wouldn't feed two growing kids for more than a few hours.

"Okay, I can see the money your father has given your mom hasn't been going to his kids, so where has it been going? I'm not trying to humiliate the two of you, but this is not at all what I'd imagined, so eat your fill, and you don't have to be polite about it." He poured tall glasses of cola from the cold two liter the delivery boy had brought with the pizza, and passed them to the kids.

"I'm going outside to make a call and if you finish eating before I get back, go pack for a couple of days, bring anything you don't want left behind because once DE gets out, you'll be living with him permanently." Eddy started to talk but Darryl held up his finger at the boy. "I said you won't be coming back and don't fuckin' argue with me, eat. I'll be right back."

He heard a soft giggle from Ginny, but acted like he hadn't heard her and walked out to the step to sit and stare at his phone for a few minutes. He found his lawyer's number. He happened to be in the same partnership with Liam's family of lawyers, and was put right through. Once Shaun Betts was informed of what Darryl wanted, he tried to talk him out of it, but Darryl insisted and Shaun told him to wait at the house with the kids.

"We have to have documentation, Darryl, we can't just grab the kids because their mother is in jail. Remember the term Due Process? You have to prove the case first, and as long as the boy who let you into the house is a resident, we can get the right people over there, give me an hour and I'll call you back."

He hated to make the next call, but John would just have to suck it up. He needed the SUV to move the kids out, and John could get his head out of his formulas and shit to come over here and help. He didn't talk to John, the message he left was short and he hoped the genius took the time to check his messages before he left the lab for the day.

His next call was to Liam, and when he answered, Darryl was so grateful that he had someone to talk to about the situation, he poured the story out as fast and as emotionless as he could manage. The rage he felt inside wasn't just directed at the kids' parents, he was pissed at himself, and guilt wasn't something he liked to feel.

Mackie put clean sheets on the beds the teens would be using, and offered to leave before they got there. "They won't understand this arrangement, and I don't know much about teenagers, but I'm pretty sure they would be confused if the three of you started kissing me whenever the whim took you, and you know I'm right, so stop shaking your head like that."

Liam grinned at her and crooked his finger. "Come with me, I want to show you something."

She had her turn at shaking her head. "Oh no you don't, big guy, I saw what you had to show me this morning, and as impressive as it is, I don't want the kiddies seeing it or my bare ass."

He laughed out loud. "Dammit, that is not what I want to show you, right now that is. You can see that anytime you like, you have my permission to molest me at anytime you feel the urge. All I ask is that you restrain your urges when my grandmother is around, it would encourage her into telling anyone in earshot of her exploits as a dancer, and it's fine to read in history books, but listening to your grandma saying that stuff is unsettling. She'd probably tell you about forgetting to put her "lacies" back on after her encounter with Sinatra, or the time a jealous rival put hot pepper juice in the rinse water of her ladies undergarments."

Mackie was holding a hand over her mouth to keep from shouting in laughter and fist pumping the air in solidarity with grandma.

"Oh sure, you can laugh, but don't do that in front of Grandmother, she would tell you how each time she would perspire while dancing, the pepper juice would leech into the sweat and cause a burning so badly that she couldn't wear clothing for a week afterwards. The old girl has no filter, she tells my father that she's earned her right to say what she wants to say."

He took her hand in his and began towing her toward the back door. "Come on, you'll enjoy this, and unless you insist, you get to keep your clothes on."

They went out to the barn and she followed him up the rough hewn steps into the loft. There was a huge apartment on the other side of the thick wooden door he pushed her through, and she turned in a circle to take it all in. Modern appliances were featured in the kitchen area, and the open space of kitchen, dining room, and living room were all visible from any spot in the room. Three doors on the left side of the loft were bedrooms and a large bathroom, all had the doors open, and the place featured canister sky lighting to save on energy throughout.

She looked at Liam, and he grinned. "I told you there was no need to panic. Darryl and the kids can take over the house, and the rest of us can enjoy the quiet if we need it."

She explored the place and turned around to say, "I love it, and you'd better watch out, if the kids are adventurous, they'll be the ones taking this place over and we'll all be shuttled off to the big house."

She considered his smile for a minute and remembered something she'd heard about teenagers. "I think we need to go back to the grocery store before they get here, I don't know much about kids like I said, but I remember being told that they'll eat anything that doesn't crawl away and isn't nailed down. I didn't see milk or cereal or—"

He interrupted her list with his lips on hers, and when he drew back he pulled her by the hand back to the stairs. "Then by all means, let's run to the store, from what John said it's an interesting place to go, and I've been wanting to see what it's like."

She was stunned, neither man had been in a grocery store? "Okay, maybe it's just me here, but why haven't you shopped for food before? I don't see a housekeeper, and yet there was food when we got here, someone had to have brought that in."

He smiled and shook his head. "Mackie, we phone the local store and everything is delivered while we're here. In town, Dorian or one of the housekeepers does the shopping. I'm too busy most of the time, and Darryl went once and brought back nothing but meat and salad stuff. He doesn't keep that body by eating what the rest of us enjoy. I admit, I work out, and have to watch what I eat at times because I've got a sweet tooth, and John is like me. Darryl usually throws out the junk food and we have to hide it so he can't."

He took her teasing him well considering. Mackie had a bit of fun ragging on him, being the tough executive who made underlings tremble in their wingtips, but "has to hide the good stuff from the mean old health food nut".

When he threatened to spank her, Mackie stuck out her tongue and laughed harder. "I'm a bit big to be spanked, and with the padding I have, you'll feel the sting in your hand worse than I would on my ass."

His answering grin made her blush. "Sugar, the point of a spanking to a woman like you wouldn't be to give you pain, I'd do it to give you pleasure, there's something about a nice pink cheeked, freshly spanked ass that makes a man want to sink his cock slow and deep, so you just keep up the teasing, and I'll keep counting the smacks I owe you."

She shifted in the seat and thought about what he said. Honesty made her reply in a matter of fact voice, and he nodded his head as she spoke. "I don't know how I would take something like that. I might hurt you if I felt pain or threatened. When I said that I can kill a man with one hand, I wasn't joking. I'd hate to end up with you dead, or in the emergency room, when all you were doing was playing or trying to give me the pleasure you're talking about."

He could see that she was serious and didn't discount her fears for his safety. "Thank you for the heads up, sugar, but I'd cut off my hand before I hurt you, anything like that would be something we can discuss and maybe in time you will feel comfortable enough to talk about the marks on your back. I won't ask you about them, and I'll be sure to tell the others you don't want to talk about it. You have all of our secrets, and I hope sooner than later you can trust us with yours."

He pulled into the supermarket parking lot. "Now, let's go inside, and you can show me what a great thing grocery shopping is." He parked the silver sports car in the back row of the lot, and they walked into the store hand in hand.

By the time they unloaded the groceries into the car, Mackie had three bags across her legs and two under them. The little car was fun to drive, impressive normally for its high performance engineering, but they found it wasn't built for a trip to the market during such an epic purchase.

The SUV was sitting out in front of the house when they got back and Darryl introduced the teens as he handed them bags of groceries from Mackie's lap. "This is Mackie, and she doesn't take smart assed shit from anyone, even me, so watch your mouths around her and she might let you live to enjoy getting to know her. Remind me to tell you about the cool stuff she can do, and the best part is I know she can do them because we all saw her do it."

What astonished her more than the words of praise was his lip-lock and, when she opened her eyes after he let her go, to see grins on the faces of the teenagers kept her wondering what he'd told them. Just to teach him a lesson, she punched him in the gut, and smiled when the girl's eyes widened and the boy shouted in laughter. Darryl's hand went to his midsection and he shot her a hurt look. "Did I hurt your feelings? I'm sorry."

She turned to the kids and held out her hand attempting to establish a friendly attitude. "Your brother is a strange duck, but I like him so I let him live because for some reason, I think I might like to get to know him better."

Ginny turned away from her hand, but Eddy came right up to her and grinned. "I see that you know how bossy my brother can be, it's about time someone gave him a good smackdown, I just met him and I've wanted to punch him at least four times." He took the bags from her hands and kept talking, "You are a tall drink of water, aren't you? He told us you were all good n' stuff, but he didn't tell me that he had such a beauty stashed away up here."

Eddy kept chatting her up and she grinned at the young man with the charm of an established teen heart throb. All the time she listened to his elaborate compliments, she thought he would be a boy the girls would fight over, once his body filled out to match his looks. She shot Darryl and Liam a look as she walked next to her new fan. Liam was rolling his eyes, and Darryl was scowling. She laughed out loud at those looks, and since Eddy thought she was laughing at one of his corny jokes, the kid puffed up his chest and tried for another laugh with yet another outrageous compliment. She was glad when they got into the house.

John took over kitchen duties with the teens doing the unpacking and putting things where he told them to put the stuff. "This way you'll know where everything is, and can help yourselves when you get hungry."

Dinner was plotted between Ginny and John, and the resulting dinner of mac and cheese with sloppy joes was a hit. Mackie shook her head in amusement when she saw that every male in the house had dribbled the red juice from the sandwiches onto the front of their shirts and ignored the spots. Ginny had delicately nibbled at the food in front of her, all the time looking as if she would fall asleep at anytime. The girl barely spoke to her after seeing the way Darryl played the victim from her earlier punch into his hard abs.

Mackie wondered how it felt to feel loyalty to someone who was a close relative but one she'd never met before. She suspected there was a deep hero-worship thing going on here. Looking at Darryl sitting between the teens and talking to them, she could see why Ginny felt that way toward her newfound big brother. He was larger than life.

The next morning, rather than take the kids to school, Darryl insisted on taking them to get new clothes and things they needed. He had a few tense minutes with Eddy, but in the end, Mackie was drafted to go with Darryl to help with "girly things".

Darryl had no idea what the girl needed, but he was counting on Mackie and told the two straight up, "I don't care how much you spend, but get rid of those baggy things that belong in a burn barrel. I want to see a happy little sister with enough bags and boxes of girl crap and clothes to outfit two fourteen year olds." He handed Mackie a credit card and pulled her close for a hug and a quick kiss, before pointing Eddy to the shoe store directly across from where they stood.

The first place they walked inside of, Mackie had to almost drag the girl inside. "Look, Darryl wants to make you happy, and from what he told me last night about the life he thought you led, and the life you actually have been living, he feels guilty for not paying attention to you for all these years. If you don't do what he is asking you to do, he's going to feel even more guilt. So this is what I think you should do. Let's teach him a lesson in how women can spend money when a man is dumb enough to say he doesn't care how much you spend."

A twenty something gum popping girl with blue streaks in her brown hair came close with a big smile. "Did I hear that right? Did he really say he didn't care? Well, sister, you came to the right place, let's see how much fun you can have spending your dad's money." She tugged Ginny through the store pulling clothes from racks as they passed and set her up in a changing room in the back of the store while she went on the hunt for more clothing to entice the shy teen. Mackie was thankful for the girl's selling technique, and sat outside the fitting room to help Ginny decide on which clothes looked best on her slender frame.

By the time they'd selected four new outfits and the belts and a hat to add to the pile, Ginny was more enthusiastic, and tossed her old clothes into a bag while she wore a new pair of jeans and a t-shirt out of the store. They hit the lingerie section hot and heavy at the next stop and Ginny looked at Mackie when she was standing in front of a display of thongs and g-strings.

Mackie knew this was a test, she wasn't sure why, but she played along. "I hate those things, and I still can't see what the big deal is. I tried them for a week and tossed them out, I mean how uncomfortable does a woman have to be? I hate that feeling of the material up the crack of my butt. I prefer a French cut or bikini cut for myself, but if those are what you like then go ahead." She turned to look at bras and noticed the girl left the sexy panties in the display alone, she turned to the next table with a rainbow of beautifully colored bikini cut panties, and began making her selections.

Shoes were selected just before noon, and Mackie couldn't resist buying two pair for herself. "Some women feel good in sexy underwear, some feel good in pretty dresses, and some, like me, feel good in a pair of nice shoes, it's my weakness, and I own too many pairs of boots and heels than I should, but I like them, I pay for them and they are my big indulgence. So you know my vice now, please don't tell Darryl or the guys, they would tease me unmercifully."

Her confession brought about the first giggle from her companion, and from then on, they began to actually talk. Ginny divulged the name of the boy in Eddy's class she had a crush on, "He doesn't know I exist, but he is the cutest, smartest guy in the whole world."

The girl was shocked when Mackie made appointments for them after lunch to have their hair cut and styled. "My mom said I didn't need to get my hair cut until I was older and boys started to notice me, she said that until then I needed to select the best boys that came from the best families, so I could marry one of them when we graduated high school."

She looked down at her feet when she said that, and Mackie asked her if she really wanted that kind of life. "Do you really want to pick out a husband from a crop of hormone riddled boys with no idea what they plan to do when they get out of college? Not to mention that if a boy gets married right out of high school nowadays, he probably won't go to college because he'll be busy working at a dead end job to support the two of you."

Ginny shook her head. "No, I mean yes I want to maybe get married, but I want to travel and I want to have a career. I think I'd like to work for Darryl, or something interesting. He said that you are a security expert person like him. He respects you a lot, and I think he loves you too. Whatever I do, I don't want to end up like my mom."

The girl shut down after that until they met Darryl and Eddy at the food court for lunch. While the teens ate foot long hot dogs and greasy fries, she got a plate of fried rice and sweet and sour chicken, which Darryl kept stealing pieces of.

The men were ready to leave, but Ginny shook her head, "But Mackie made us hair appointments and," she shut up and began plucking at the pepperoni on her plate.

Mackie shot him an evil glare, and Darryl shrugged his shoulders. "Well go for it, we can hang out at the sporting goods place next door, just text me when you're ready to go."

When they finally got out of the beauty salon, Darryl smiled, and it was Eddy's turn to scowl. He said under his breath, "Damn, now I'm going to have to bust some heads at school, the first guy I see hitting on my little sister will be sorry."

Chapter 17

The teens were with them for the rest of the week, and everyone hugged it out as Darryl and Liam loaded the SUV to take them back to their father's house. It was amazing to see the massive amount of things the kids had collected from all of the adults in the house. John had taken Ginny to the kitchen supply store and had come back with boxes and boxes of kitchen gadgets and special pans. The two of them had been watching cooking shows, and she had abandoned her thoughts of going to work with Darryl. She now wanted to be a chef, so John did his best to make sure she could indulge in her new hobby. He took Eddy with him to get the tools of every teenaged boy's "boy's junk" as Ginny called it. Including bats, balls, a mitt, and new running shoes. Liam wasn't about to be out done, and just before they closed the back of the SUV, he added a game system with several games and accessories.

That night, the house seemed empty, and finally Mackie had enough of the gloomy faces. They had all been very careful around the kids, and she decided it was time to talk. The week had been a great way to get to know each other. The tenderness each man had displayed even when they would rather not be interrupted by noise from the yelling kids, told her everything she needed to know about them.

She found them hiding out in the weight room in the basement twice, and laughed at the relieved expressions when she told them the kids went to bed for the night.

It was time for her to tell them her story in its entirety. If they still wanted to make the relationship work, she planned to love these men with everything she had inside of herself. If they couldn't see their way to wanting her after she told them, then she would start her life over with a broken heart, but she would survive.

They were all sitting around the living room talking about the workload for the upcoming week when she brought in two bottles of wine and glasses for all of them to enjoy. She set the tray down and opened the first bottle, poured each of them a glass and handed them around, before sitting down on the floor opposite where they sat.

"So, it's been quite a week, and I think I'll miss the noise." Groans followed her words from the men, but she smiled and took a sip of her wine before she set it down and sat up straight. "I think you guys should know who I am, so I'm putting it all out for you.

"My birth name is Maxine Timmons. I was placed in a foster home when my parents were killed in a drug raid at the house we lived in when I was eight years old. The foster home was great, but three days after my tenth birthday, I was pulled off my bike by a man named Renaldo. I was taken to a place where they manufactured and packaged cocaine, and sometimes heroin." She took a sip of the blood red wine, and swallowed it past the dryness of her mouth. "I was forced to help other children package the stuff for the pushers to sell, and the day I arrived, they beat me bloody to make me understand that there was only one way out, and that was if I was dead."

She didn't look at the men while she spoke. They remained silent, so she continued her story. "Four of the children died while I was there, but I can't remember much about them. One night, just before dark, after we finished packaging up four bricks of coke, we were sent to our room. We started to hear gunshots and shouting. The quiet afterwards was eerie. The two girls that were with me and I stayed huddled in a corner for probably an hour after the shooting, waiting to see if we were next, but no one came. I got up and peeked around the door, and all of our captors were dead except for one, it was Renaldo, and he was limping around gathering a bag full of cash and drugs before he snuck out of the place."

She sipped a few more swallows of her drink and continued her tale of being frightened, and helping the twins return to their hometown. She looked directly at Liam when she explained how she hooked up with Louisa, and once she was finished telling them, she got up and reached for the bottle to refill her drink. She changed her mind in mid reach, and instead set the glass on the table before turning to walk out of the room. "I need to take a walk, I'll be back, but right now, I need to be alone." She kept walking and left the house, quietly closing the door behind herself. She felt raw inside, and she needed to sit in the fresh air for a while. Sometimes when things got overwhelming, she had to go outside and breathe.

John spoke after the outer door could be heard opening and closing. "Was that her way of telling us that she feels stifled? Or did she just bare her darkest secrets because she finally made a decision? I can understand how her life must seem to a young girl that other people might judge, but what she told us hasn't changed my mind about her one bit."

Liam nodded his head in agreement. To think that this woman had gone through such a childhood, and came out like the smart, talented women she was now, gave him an even deeper sense of pride in his choice of woman to be the one for them. "She's a survivor, and what's the bet that when those children were huddled in that corner of the room, she was shielding the other two? Can you imagine the courage that took for a kid her age?"

Darryl agreed with everything the others said, and wanted to add more praise for the little girl who had come from hell and survived the test each time life threw one at her. He didn't bother to say the things that boiled in his gut to be said. Liam and John weren't the ones that needed to hear what he had to say— Mackie was. "You know the way she acted with the teens tells me she would be a bitch on wheels if she had kids of her own. We'd never have to worry they would be neglected or left with someone just for her convenience. The kids might feel like Mommy was overprotective, but God help anyone who hurt them." He grinned at his companions. "Can you imagine her as an archangel complete with a sword to smite the bullies?"

The answering grins and possible scenarios filtered through their minds. Each man nodded almost in sync. They knew she was the one to complete their circle. Now it was up to her.

Mackie walked through the field thinking about her life. She had never told anyone about the last night at the drug house, even the shrink. Remembering the look on her friend's face in death still gave her a sense of purpose when she was protecting clients, but she'd often wondered over the years who would stand up for her if she needed a hero. Picturing the three of them in tights and capes made her smile through watery eyes.

The three men back at the house had given her an option. She could take the chance on them, and be the woman they needed, or she could leave and stay gone. Monday would bring normal back into their lives, and she had no idea what she would do with her life if she did leave. They seemed to believe that she was worth the risks they were taking and truthfully, she had nothing to lose by loving them except her heart.

Well, you've never played it safe before, and look at what you stand to gain by staying. She nodded to herself and turned back, intending to tell them of her decision, and unless they changed their minds, she would be walking into her future.

They met her at the door when she walked in. "Where's the fire?" got looks of relief, and she knew they were coming to find her. Knowing they worried made her heart feel like it was growing, and she shook her head at them. "I told you I'd be back, sometimes emotional shit makes me crave fresh air, and I have to walk the feelings out."

She had trouble finding something generic to say, the awkward silence as they all stood staring at each other made her nervous, she didn't meant to blurt out, "I've thought about my decision whether to stay and be with you all, or should I leave. I decided that if you still want to make a life between us, then, let's do it. I don't know how, but if we all work at it, and communicate, we should be able to pull it off."

John put his arm around her waist and urged her further into the living room. Liam handed her a glass of wine when she was finally seated between John and Darryl on the couch, and he sat on the table in front of them. He picked her feet up and set them on his knees while he took her shoes and socks off. He began rubbing her feet and she moaned from his firm massage on her feet that had never felt such bliss before.

"That's what I'm talking about, how many women have three handsome sexy beasts at her beck and call?" Liam smiled at his description but sobered when he continued to talk, "Mackie, I swear I will do my best to make your life happy and anything you want, you will have if it's in my power to give you. We talked while you went on your walk, and we all feel the same. Give us a chance and we'll prove it to you."

Darryl and John were nodding their heads and murmuring *yes*, while she sat enjoying her feet being massaged and staring into the wine in her glass. They seemed to be waiting for her to say something, and all she could think was that she was the one who had been blessed after so many years of being alone.

"Look, this can't be just you guys breaking your necks to make me happy, I've been alone pretty much my entire life. I've had passing relationships that lasted a day or two, but I never had the urge to settle down with anyone before. You have each other, and I—that first night, I watched you making love. It was the singular most beautiful thing I'd ever witnessed. I wanted to be included in that caring.

"Since then I've watched you squabble like siblings, I've seen the way Darryl went into attack mode when you were in danger. John was just as upset and ready to run in there regardless of what those men planned to do if they had gotten their hands on him. I know that you, Liam, stared at the door for half an hour after Darryl left to straighten out his family problems. You looked like you wanted to follow him, but resigned to staying here while your buddy took care of things on his own. I've never had that, and I want it, you have no idea how badly I want to belong to someone who cares about me as much as I care about them.

"Just love me, that's all I need. That's all anybody really needs, people that love them. I want it, and in return, I'll do anything I can to keep you happy."

John said what the men were thinking, and they nodded their heads as he said, "Just be you, sugar, be the brave beautiful person who we all love, you won't regret putting your trust in our hands. You had us the minute you stood there ready to shoot Liam over a punch. Our own personal one woman army, what man can resist a woman with beauty, brains, and those fun things that go boom?"

Mackie laughed out loud at his description of her remembering what Thom had said all of those months past. He told her men had a hard time resisting toys that she had an affinity with, and it struck her sense of ridiculous. The men looked at her questioning, but she was laughing too hard to explain, maybe someday she would, but this wasn't the day. She looked at John and said, "I need a shower."

He grinned and stood to pull her to her feet and lead her to the shower. The half glass of wine was set down on the vanity, and he slowly stripped the clothing from her body with her assistance. He stripped his clothes off while she soaked her hair and washed the long strands. His hands took over rinsing and conditioning her hair, and he soaped her body down with the puff, paying special attention to her breasts, and the crease of her pussy and ass. He placed her hand on his shoulder for balance when he knelt to shave the lips of her cunt and used one finger to travel over every inch to make sure there were no stray hairs left behind. By the time he had rinsed her pink flesh for the last time, her creamy liquids continued to slide from her body, and her clit was hard and begging for his lips to give her another orgasm. Instead of pleasuring her this time, he turned off the water and stepped out of the shower stall to grab a towel for her hair, which she used to dry the wet mess while he dried her body with another thinner towel that sucked the water droplets from her body faster than his lips and tongue licked and sucked them away. They walked naked to the room at the end of the hall, and Mackie wasn't surprised to see the biggest bed she'd ever seen sitting in the middle of the room. There was a vanity table with a stool for her to sit at, and he began detangling her hair while she sat enjoying the pampering.

"This feels so good, I love it." GreyC came closer, jumped onto her lap, and began batting at John's fingers as he tried to run the brush through the wet strands of hair.

Darryl entered the room damp and naked, with Liam following him mere seconds later. Both of their cocks were semi hard in anticipation of what was to come, and she admired her men as they walked past where she sat. The cat wasn't looking friendly, but she curled up on her lap and enjoyed the ear scratching Mackie gave her while John took his time with her hair.

Darryl grinned at the picture and said, "Isn't that a pretty picture, a pussy on a pussy. The furball is more than a pretty face, soft fur and mouse killing abilities, she's keeping our meal warm until we're ready to eat it. Good, kitty."

Mackie rolled her eyes and had to grin at his goofy joke. John braided her hair and finished it off with a small hair tie from the package on the vanity. She could feel his cock nudging at her spine and she wanted to see it, so she turned around and reached for the smooth shaft before he could pull back from her hand. She gave him a narrow eyed look, and he shrugged.

Her fingers slid up and down the smooth skin and she couldn't resist leaning down to lick the satin flesh covering the head of his cock. The dark pink color invited her to taste more of him, and she indulged her senses by taking him into her moist mouth. Her tongue tested the textures and licked away the small drop of pre-cum that escaped from his restraint. When she made a satisfied *hmmm* sound in her throat, she felt him jerk his hips, but she refused to let him loose from the captivity of her mouth. *Oh no*, she had him and she planned to keep him right there.

Hands reached over her shoulders and took her hard nipples between fingers and thumbs, and she moaned again. The increasing pressure on the small buds made her gasp, and as soon as her mouth opened to take in a deeper breath, he pulled his cock from between her lips.

Lips caressed the nape of her neck and she shivered. Soft words with equally soft breaths whispering against the still damp hair at her temple brought another delicious shiver and moan that she couldn't stop from escaping, and didn't really want to try to stop it.

"Come on, sugar, let's get you over on the bed." Liam's voice was seducing her as much as his lick to her jawline. She didn't expect him to lift her into his arms and carry her to the bed with almost no effort. She was afraid to move in case she overbalanced him or something, but he handed her over to Darryl.

She was flipped onto the bed, and before she got her breath back, Darryl had her knees separated and was smiling into her eyes as he slowly lowered his head to the soaked lips of her pussy. His lips latched onto her clit and sealed around the hooded muscle. When he began sucking strongly, and letting the suction lessen, and then repeating the caress several times, she felt the way his tongue slapped at the tiny muscle that emerged from the hood of flesh. His teeth lightly scraped over her clit and she screamed between her gritted teeth, arching her back to invite his mouth onto further territory. His lips stayed glued to her clit, but his hands wrapped around each thigh, and she found herself straddling his head with her knees spread as wide as possible, and his tongue continuing to torture the muscle between his teeth.

Fingers entered her and she jerked each time the fingers slid in and out. Darryl's hands were holding the cheeks of her ass wide and when the fingers left her pussy and began probing at her asshole, she raised her bent head and cried out, and grabbed her breasts. Pinching the nipples and twisting them to the point of pain as she came unglued to the pleasure she felt. She felt the spasms of her inner muscles and screamed, grinding her pussy over the mouth that continued to wring every drop of pleasure from her that it could.

Hands urged her to crawl backwards on her knees off Darryl's face, and over his chest to pause above the long, thick cock that was waiting impatiently to slide deep inside of her wet heat.

She slid down over his cock and hissed at the fullness stretching her inner muscles that were still tingling from her first orgasm. His hips and hands lifted her body and worked to seat his cock deep, and he held her hips down on his for several seconds to allow her body to adjust to his size.

"Hang on, sugar, I'm with you, but if you move right now, I'll be finished before I begin. Your pussy is so damn tight, I love the way it squeezes my cock, but we," her inner muscles began to clench over his cock, and he gritted his teeth. He turned his head and saw John watching, stroking his cock.

"Do something, man, she's clamping down and I'm ready to explode."

It wasn't John who slid his lubed finger into her asshole. Liam distracted her in a big way even as he pinched Darryl's nutsac and pulled on it, to prolong his performance. It distracted Darryl enough to slow the urge to slam his hips up and his cock deeper while she reached for her next orgasm. Darryl had to close his eyes to the sight of Mackie's face, as Liam replaced his fingers with his cock in her asshole. He felt the hard cock enter her tight ass, and every inch that penetrated pushed against his through the thin membrane of skin between her pussy and ass. "Fuck, so fucking good. How are you doing, sugar? You doin' okay there?"

Mackie was panting through the feeling of having her asshole penetrated for the first time with anything larger than a finger, and the burning slightly painful stretch of her rear entrance combined with the clenching of her vaginal muscles overwhelmed her senses. She wanted whatever this feeling was to keep growing and she began working her own hips to take one, and keep the other cock buried deep.

She leaned down further to kiss and bite at Darryl's lips and neck when John's cock touched her cheek. His hand held a fistful of her hair. "This time just lick my cock, sugar, I'm ready to come, but you're clenching your teeth, and I want to keep my cock attached to me. Can you do that, beauty?" She whimpered, and stretched her tongue out to touch the dark pink flesh, and he let her head lower, but kept alert for her orgasm, because she was pumping her hips harder on the cocks filling her, and *Ah, right there*, he could see her eyes glaze over and the shiver indicating her pleasure was peeking. Her mouth opened as a scream escaped, and her fingers dug into Darryl's shoulders. He pulled his hips back to get his cock out of the way of her sharp teeth until she relaxed enough to assure him that she was calm enough to continue licking and sucking his now ready to explode cock.

Her body continued to clench and shiver from the aftershocks of the best orgasm she'd ever experienced. Liam's and Darryl's cocks filled her so well that she received a smaller orgasm as she felt them coming inside of her body. The hot liquid filling her caused her sensitive tissues to keep her on edge for that moment, and she closed her eyes, floating along in pleasure like she'd never known. When she opened her eyes, John's cock was within kissing distance, and she angled her head over enough to kiss and lick the cum droplets from his beautiful offering. She didn't attempt to stop the purring sound that vibrated from her throat onto his cock.

John's cock rested across Darryl's lips and hers, she began kissing the top side of his cock, while Darryl licked the front side. They shared the delicious treat of his flesh, and when John could hold back no longer, his fist clenched the pillows as he shuttled his cock between the two sets of lips and when he came they licked each other's cheeks clean and wiped the cum from their chins. They were grinning at each other by the time his cock was allowed to leave the clutches of their mouths, and John shook his head at the way they played with him, keeping his flesh hard and sensitive for long minutes.

"That was mean, but so damn good." He leaned down and kissed each of them in turn. "Remind me to return the favor next time."

Liam's spent cock left her body, and she shivered again, but the kisses he laid down the column of her spine was what caused that. She stayed sprawled on top of Darryl until Liam and John left the bed, and they hauled her up and over his hips to lie next to the big man. It was a good thing they were there to help because her legs didn't want to function like they should, and those delicious tremors deep inside of her body continued for long moments after they disentangled from each other.

John left the room and came back a few minutes later to pull her from the bed and into the bathroom where a deep tub of hot water was filling for her to enjoy.

"Oh you know the way to a woman's heart alright." She took his cheeks between her palms and kissed him, before stepping into the swirling water.

Chapter 18

The next morning over coffee and toast, Darryl told them about what happened when he took the kids home to their father.

"The old man had tears when the kids hugged him. I didn't get it, until they all told me about the cousin Chrissy hooked up with after her and DE broke up. The guy has a gambling problem, and both of them are addicts. They bled DE dry, and his business is in big trouble. She held the kids hostage, and he paid her until there was nothing left to

pay. That's why he kept calling me for money."

Liam spoke, "How much do you need to buy into the business? I'm telling you right now, I don't trust the man, I don't give a damn what his story is. I'll float the loan, and take fifty-one percent of the business if he defaults. The rest of it will be held for the kids when they reach maturity. It'll be a personal loan, Klinger's won't be involved. That way he has to answer to someone else, not his own son. If I know you, you'd let him get away with fucking you over, I'm not as kind-hearted as you are. If it wasn't for the kids, I'd say fuck him, let him rot in poverty, but I like the brats, and I love you."

As they discussed the loan and the business side of such a loan, John came up behind her and rubbed her shoulders. She put her hand over one of his and leaned her head back onto his stomach. This place, these men, she could see them all together now. It wouldn't always be this easy, but where there was love, there was a family.

When Darryl declared that she would be involved in the security business with him to, "Keep you occupied and out of trouble," made her feel part of the team, and she grinned when Liam demanded that she be his bodyguard when he traveled overseas.

GreyC jumped onto her favorite man of the day's lap, who happened to be Liam, and bit the hand that stopped petting her to get his attention. Everyone smiled as he resumed her massage.

How she got so lucky was beyond her comprehension, but looking at the three men who'd changed her life and given her a place to be herself, all she had to do was love them, the love part was easy, the rest would work itself out.

Lynn Ray Lewis

I love writing Erotic Fiction.
Give me peace and quiet or a set of
headphones and a good music library and i will
write until my hands hurt. Then I will lay in bed
and think of what my characters will do or say
next.

By Lynn Ray Lewis

Jody's Men
Regina's Men
Mackie's Men
Lucy's Men

A Place For Her (Hade's Temple Book 1)

I Waited For You (Gaurdians Book 1)

Rane's Giants (Tremble Island Book 1)
Hawk's Nest (Tremble Island Book 2)
Demon's End (Tremble Island Book 3)